SOPHIE WAS VIOLENTLY JEALOUS OF HER OWN SISTER

Sophie and Sarah were identical in looks—but Sophie was sharply aware of how different she was from her sister, and keenly wished it were not so.

Sarah was always calm and in control—and Sophie ever quick to yield to her feelings, and then to regret her surrender.

Sarah never swerved from her love for one man alone—while Sophie found romance to be a bewitching, bewildering maze.

Sarah was clearly running no risk of disaster—while Sophie was gambling all her happiness and honor itself in a game with two suitors.

There was the good and faithful Oliver and the powerful and persuasive Earl of Leighton—and Sophie had no idea whom she wanted to win.

Also by Margaret SeBastian:

HER KNIGHT ON A BARGE   04399 $1.75

THE HONORABLE MISS CLARENDON   04304 $1.75

LORD DEDRINGHAM'S DIVORCE   04248 $1.75

This offer expires 1/25/81   8999

BYWAY TO LOVE

Margaret SeBastian

FAWCETT COVENTRY • NEW YORK

BYWAY TO LOVE

Published by Fawcett Coventry Books, a unit of CBS Publications, the Consumer Publishing Division of CBS Inc.

ISBN: 0-449-50044-6

Printed in the United States of America

First Fawcett Coventry printing: May 1980

10   9   8   7   6   5   4   3   2   1

BYWAY TO LOVE

Chapter 1

Sophie and Sarah Sandringham were seated together in the small parlor that overlooked Cavendish Square. They had all the appearance of a pair of contented kittens as they sat and prosed away in the sunlit room.

Their resemblance to each other was truly remarkable, and if they had been dressed in identical gowns, a stranger would never have been sure that he was not troubled with double vision. But, fortunately for any such stranger, Sarah was garbed in pale blue and Sophie was garbed in pale yellow, although the cut and style of their morning dresses were very similar. It was upon this very subject of dress that they were discoursing.

Said Sarah: "It comes to me, my dear, that we

have got to stay with a particular color once we have worn it, and that seems to me to be something of a bore."

"I have been thinking along that line, too. But surely we do not have to stay with the *same* color. Why can we not wear any hue we choose except that one of us always makes sure it is light in shade whereas the other selects only the deeper shades, color alike or no?"

"Oh, but the deeper shades do not go at all well with us. We are so fair to begin with that we should be absolutely livid in contrast. No, I have got a better idea. We can do what other females do, select costumes that suit us whatever they may be, color or cut. We must just be sure never to wear the same things at the same time."

"Why, yes, and I can see how that might work out very well for us. If we never purchase two costumes that are alike, so long as we select from our common wardrobe, we can never appear dressed alike. It will not be at all difficult. In fact, I think I am going to like it. We have been twins far too long, I am thinking, and, while we have had loads of fun at it, it has finally caught up with us with a vengeance! Oh, I still shudder all over when I recall how strange Oliver looked when I asked him if he was sure it was I who he addressed instead of you. I assure you it quite broke my heart. I knew on the instant that it was he I loved—which only made matters worse, of course."

"Yes: I know precisely what you mean. It was

quite the same for Percy, the poor dear. Oh, how could we have been so cruel!"

"Well, it all turned out quite well in the event, and I am not going to brood on what is past. They have forgiven us, and that is all that matters."

"Yes, and I say we owe a debt of gratitude to Alan for straightening the matter out. I am sure I had not the faintest idea of how to go about it. An apology, no matter how humbly offered, would never have been sufficient."

"Indeed, I am so happy we married Pennie to Alan."

Sarah chuckled. "He has paid us back in our own coin and is bound not to let us forget it. Well, I dare say that our loves must be very close to home by this time. Oh, I do hope that they do not have trouble locating Papa. If only he is still holding court in Loughborough, it will make things so easy."

"Well, I am sure that our lads will seek him out. They both of them are used to the Chase and, even if they are not very clever about finding their way in London, they have never had the least trouble in Leicestershire. Why, they know Charley Forest as well as I know the back of my hand."

"You do not think that Papa will have any objections to our engagement, do you?"

"It is not Papa that I am worried about. It is Mama. She has never looked upon either Percy or Oliver as being numbered amongst the brightest— but, then, she does not truly know them, does she?"

"No, it is truly their fault. If they would stop

their eternal bickering with each other, then people might have a chance to see them in their true colors, I am sure. But what of their parents? That is going to be a bit sticky, I think, especially for Oliver."

Sophie frowned and nodded. "That is true, but Percy may not find things so easy, either."

"I know," said Sarah, sadly. "Not only must he try for the viscount's approval of his engagement, but he has the further task of seeking his approval of his new post with Alan. Oh, it would be so nice if Percy could take the position of Alan's clerk. Just imagine! My Percy studying under a judge of King's Bench Court. Why, that must be the most preeminent court in the land!"

"It must be if its lord chief justice is the lord chief justice of England. You know, I would not be surprised if our brother-in-law would succeed to that exalted honor eventually."

"Was there ever an earl who became lord chief justice before?"

"I have not the faintest idea, but I'll take my oath that our lady sister never thought she was getting a high judge when she married herself an earl."

"With our help, one might add."

"I think we had better have very little to say about that in the future, for the fun of it is beginning to wear a bit thin with Alan. I am sure he would fain believe he did it all himself."

"And he has paid us back right well— Oh, I do hope that the viscount will not put any objections in Percy's way! He does have his heart set on entering the legal profession and, with Alan's help, he is bound to rise quickly—not that he could not do it on his own, you will understand—but to have the earl of Dalby at your back is not to be sneezed at."

"Still, Sarah, Percy has it much easier than my Oliver. Mr. Grantford was never the friendliest sort, and he has been on the outs with Oliver forever! Oh, if only Oliver had applied himself in school, he and his father would have been so much more a proper father and son. Think of it! Oliver has got to ask his father to repay all that Percy has laid out for him. I think it is a shame when a father cannot provide a proper allowance to his son so that he can be free to travel as he wills."

"I am thankful that Percy is not down with *that* complaint. He has his own fortune, you know."

"Yes, I know," said Sophie, a little bitterly. "And that is what makes it so awful, for even though Percy's father is a viscount, Oliver's father could buy him out with the least lightening of his pocket."

"Oh, dearest, I am sure it will not turn out badly."

"But what if it should? Percy could still marry you, whatever his father had to say to it. He has an independence and a post, thanks to Alan, but my poor Oliver must depend upon Mr. Grantford for every penny."

"Sophie, you just must not think like that! Dear, I can assure you it will all turn out for the best."

"That is quite easy for you to say. *I* am not so sure."

"Well, it is fool's work to continue in this vein, I

am sure. Let us pass on to something more pleasant."

"Yes, for it is quite putting me into the mopes. So we are agreed that all we need do to avoid all confusion is to wear something different, never to dress alike again."

"Yes. It is quite a simple thing to do. In fact, the very first thing, we must go through our wardrobe and discard one of any two that are alike. Then we should have no further difficulty on that score."

"But, Sarah, that will amount to half our clothing!" objected Sophie.

Sarah grinned. "Yes, won't it though! Pennie shall just have to help us shop for more."

"But what will Alan have to say to it? It is all out of his pocket, you know."

"Well, he it was who lectured us on playing it on the square with the world. It seems perfectly fair to me that if we take his advice, he cannot complain if he is the one who pays the piper."

"The couturiere, you mean, don't you?"

They both chortled for a bit and then went on chatting.

Chapter 2

Earlier that morning, a post chaise was rattling along at a furious clip, having just gotten clear of London traffic. It was headed north and contained two young gentlemen, each of whom was too occupied with his thoughts to mind the jostling of the vehicle. The one, somewhat shorter and stockier, was leaning back in his seat, a beatific smile on his face as he contemplated his future. The other, darker and taller, was leaning forward, his elbows on his knees, swaying with the carriage, his face clouded, his look uncertain. Plainly, he was not happy. He glanced at his companion's smiling countenance, and his look grew blacker. He let out an oath and brought his fist down upon a well-tailored knee.

The honorable Percy Deverill's complacent smile faded to be replaced by a look of worry.

"I say, Oliver, what is wrong?"

"It is no good, Percy! I tell you it is no good at all!"

"Your governor? Is that what has got your wind up, old chap?"

"Aye, and more than that!"

"Now, come you! Here you are engaged to be wed to the most beautiful girl in the world and you have a face like that? Nonsense! Look upon—"

"You think that Sophie is more beautiful than Sarah?" asked Oliver in amazement.

"Well, of course I do not! The thing of it is that as Sophie is the spitting image of my Sarah, she has to be just as beautiful, does she not? Truly, there is naught to choose between the ladies for looks, you will agree."

Oliver smiled his agreement.

"Now, there's a good chap! Try to take it all a bit easier. I say, if it would help, I shall be glad to stand beside you when you beard your governor."

"Thank you, Percy, but I am sure I can handle that end of the business. At least I hope I can—but, it is not that that is disturbing me at this particular moment. It is the girls."

"Well, I must say they always disturbed *me!* Since I was twelve, I am sure!"

"No, you idiot, I am not referring to that! I am speaking of this last escapade of theirs. You know, it shook me up something fearful. Imagine going up to a female, saying all sorts of sweet nothings to her, only to find out she isn't your particular dear delight but your best chum's. I say, this sort of thing might go on for all of our lives."

"But the thing is you were right. She was just up to her usual mischief with her sister. After all, did I not go through the same business with Sarah? She has assured me that it will never happen again, and there were the tears of sincerity in her eyes when she said so, too."

"Well, Sophie said as much to me as well—but it still does not mean that they or we are in the clear over the business. With our wives looking so much alike, there is bound to be a most serious state of confusion in our breasts forever. As long as we are aware that the sister of our wife is within eye's reach, does it not seem to you that you would have to exercise the greatest caution before addressing your wife for the simple reason that you cannot be sure it *is* your wife whom you are addressing. For heaven's sake, Percy, just think of it! Just suppose they should take it into their heads to switch places at the altar. Ye gods! What an awful prospect! No one would know who married whom, by damn!"

Percy's features blanched, and now he looked as worried as did Oliver.

"Oliver, you have not changed a bit. I thought surely now that you were sure of Sophie's affection, you would not be so down upon everything. Have your opinions taken such a permanent hold of you that you can no longer see the bright side of things even when it threatens to blind you with its brilliance?"

"My friend, I am not asking you to join in with me. Just you see things your way and allow me my way. I see stormy weather ahead for the both of us if the girls ever take it into their heads to kick up their heels and play their usual tricks upon us."

"You have already said as much. It gets no better for repetition," pointed out Percy, growing morose. "I do wish you would keep it all to yourself. Now you have got me beside myself with worry."

"There, you see! The problem will not go away. Oh, you can hide from it for a time, but when you think of the prank that the girls played upon us and Fallon and Blessingame at Lady Haversham's, you can no longer have any confidence in them. Why did they have to be twins! It would have been so much easier if they had just been sisters!"

"Well, Sarah promised—"

"Bah! So did Sophie—but you know what they are!"

"I most certainly do. They are the dearest pair of females that I have—"

"Oh, do shut up! That is not what I am talking about, and you know it!"

"Well, blast, suppose that they are bound to act up a bit at first. They will settle down at last, and we shall have peace in the end. I think, for the privilege of having them for spouses, it is little enough to bear."

"Well, it happens that I do not! I am sure I should be eaten up with jealousy, never knowing for sure who you were holding in your arms, Sophie or Sarah."

"Blast you! It will be Sarah, or I'll damn well know the reason why!"

Oliver turned in his seat and pointed an emphatic finger at Percy.

"Precisely! That is exactly my point! Why? Because they are pleased to tease us. That is something they have never refrained from doing at the slightest opportunity and ever since we were children playing together. I have seen nothing to indicate that they have changed."

Said Percy, weakly: "But it is different now. They are in love with us."

"Oh, do not go all over teary-eyed with me! You have got to face the facts, man! The girls are not to be trusted!"

"The devil you say!" exploded Percy, angrily.

"The devil I *do* say!" retorted Oliver, just as fiercely.

"Then, what in blazes do you intend to do about it?" demanded Percy.

"I shall tell you what I intend to do about it!"

"Tell me, then!"

"I am backing out!"

Percy gasped and fell back into his seat. "You are mad!"

"Perhaps I am! Perhaps it is better to be mad now than to be driven mad by a wife I cannot trust!"

"Oliver, I beg you to consider what you are saying. Sophie loves you! Have you not the least faith in her?"

"Every faith except for the fact that I cannot tell her apart from Sarah."

"Oh, for God's sake, have we not been all through that? You most certainly can!"

"Well, I was not so sure of myself at Lady Haversham's party, I can tell you."

"But that is over and done with. We have the girls' words on it."

"Oh, leave me be! It is all over for me. You do what you wish."

"Are you not going to speak to your father?"

"How can I when I am so unsure of the business. Tell me, Percy, are you so bloody sure that Sarah cannot and will not fool you?"

Percy acted as though he had been pressed against a wall. He was unable, in all honesty, to speak.

Oliver, seeing his advantage, pressed home. "There! You are not so sure of her as you pretend! I tell you, Percy, we could be making the greatest mistake of our lives to go through with this."

Still Percy had nothing to say. He just sat and stared out the window of the carriage.

"Marry in haste and repent at leisure," quoted Oliver.

Finally Percy turned and asked: "Have you no love for Sophie?"

"You know I do, and that is why I think it best not to proceed with it. It must make us both unhappy in the end."

"But that must go for Sarah and me, too."

"That is your business, not mine."

"Perhaps—just perhaps, we are taking our fences too fast. Perhaps," said Percy, "just perhaps, we ought to talk it over again with the girls—to make doubly sure that all is clear between us."

"You do what you think best. In any case, it must be obvious that we have got to go back to town. There is hardly any point to continuing on."

"I dare say. Give the post boy the signal to turn back. I have not the heart."

Chapter 3

Sophie and Sarah, their morning chat at an end, decided it was time to look in upon their sister Pennie, the countess of Dalby, and had just risen from their chairs when they saw a post chaise draw up before the house. They turned to study it and gasped in unison as they witnessed Oliver and then Percy step down out of it.

"But what can they be doing back at this time? They ought to have been halfway to Leicestershire!" exclaimed Sophie.

"Surely they could not have forgotten something so important as to have made them turn back!" said Sarah.

"Oh, dear, they must have had one of their interminable arguments, they are both looking so very determined. What do you think may have happened between them?"

"Well, we shall soon learn. They are coming in. Come, let us go to greet them and see what this is all about."

They left the front parlor and stepped into the corridor leading to the front door just as it was opened by a footman, allowing the loves of their lives to come bursting in. Rather it was Oliver who came in quickly. Percy seemed to dawdle a bit.

"Ah, there you are!" cried Oliver on spying the twins. "We have got to talk to you!"

"Why, whatever is the matter?" inquired Sophie, all curiosity. "Have you and Percy had a falling out?"

"No, it is nothing like that. We have got to talk to *you!*"

"Very well. Come into the parlor," said Sophie. "I cannot imagine what could be so important that you must come all the way back from Leicestershire to say it to us."

As she spoke, she and Sarah led the way into the parlor, and everyone but Oliver took a seat. He stood and stared at Percy in indignation.

"Really, Percy, this is no time to be sitting at your ease."

"Why the devil not? I know about what you are going to say and I am not at all that much in favor of it."

"The devil you say! You did not demur when I ordered the chaise to turn back."

"Well, what could I say with you hammering

away at me like that? It would have been the devil's own game to have continued on. Go on! Speak your piece and have done with it! Then, perhaps, we can continue on to Leicestershire."

"What is your hurry? I thought we agreed that there was no point in continuing on?"

"I know I did—but it is one thing to see one's misery magnified in a cold damp carriage, whereas it is quite another thing to say as much, here in the sight of our ladies whom I happen to love dearly."

"Oliver!" gasped Sophie, very shocked.

Oliver snarled at Percy: "Now, see what you have done, you simpleton. You have shaken my lady!"

"Well, damn and blast! It was what you were going to do, was it not? What difference who begins it? At least now she is prepared."

"Oliver, I demand to know what this is all about!" exclaimed Sophie, her temper heating.

"Well, now, my dear, it is nothing at all like Percy is hinting—"

"Oliver, blast you, it was all your idea!" exclaimed Percy. "Now, you have brought us back to London, and it is your time to speak!"

"Well, if you will allow me to get a word in edgewise, my loquacious friend, I will say what it is I have got to say!"

"Then stop shilly-shallying about and say it, man!"

"Percy, stop ragging Oliver and let him speak!" commanded Sarah.

"Thank you, my dear," said Oliver with a little bow of gratitude.

"Oliver, stop making eyes at my sister and get on with it. Gracious to heaven but it can hardly be of so much moment if it takes you so much effort to get it out."

"Well, stab me if I am about to say anything at all!" exclaimed Oliver. "Everyone wishes to speak, so I shall just hold my tongue and bide my time."

"Oh, you can be so exasperating!" exclaimed Sophie.

"I am beginning to suspect that he has changed his mind," muttered Percy.

"Well, *you* seem to have."

"Do you mean to stand there and tell me that we have wasted a perfectly good fare? Why, we might have been halfway home by this time had we continued on!"

"Have no fear, tight-pockets, I shall refund you my share of the expense."

"Tight-pockets, is it? Why, you ungrate—"

At that point, Lady Dalby came into the room and the backbiting ceased as the two gentlemen saluted her.

"Oliver! Percy! Have you not started? I should have thought that you would be halfway to Leicestershire by this time—but I see a chaise at the curb—and you look as though you have been traveling. In heaven's name tell me, what brought you back?"

Percy looked to Oliver. "Will you tell her ladyship or shall I?"

"You do and I shall mill you down to a fine powder!" exclaimed Oliver, looking very embarrassed.

"Well, I do declare!" exclaimed Lady Dalby, looking at her sisters. They, in turn, shook their heads, to indicate their complete lack of understanding of what was going on.

Lady Dalby took a seat and studied Oliver, who shifted about uneasily under her gaze.

"Oliver, something is wrong, is it not? You are having second thoughts. Is that it?"

Oliver nodded.

"Oh, Oliver!" cried Sophie, and tears started to stream down her cheeks.

The sight completely unmanned Oliver, and he dropped to his knee beside her.

"I was only thinking of you, my sweet," he pleaded as he took out his handkerchief and handed it to her.

She patted at her eyes, sniffed and asked: "What were you thinking?"

"That I could never be sure it was you after we were married. So you can see how deucedly difficult it would be for all concerned."

Sophie stood up, gave him a withering look and announced: "I am going to my room!"

She started to stalk out, but Lady Dalby said, quietly: "Young lady, kindly resume your seat. I did not give you leave."

"But, Pennie, you heard him—"

"Sophie!"

Sophie made a face, her dramatic exit in a shambles, and came back to her chair.

"Now, then, Oliver, I think you are being utterly nonsensical about the matter. Tell me, do you love Sophie?"

He nodded doggedly.

"And tell me further, do you believe that Sophie loves you?"

He nodded again and looked down at his hands.

"Then you cannot possibly believe what you have been saying. It is, indeed, something else that has your wind up, is it not?"

He hesitated for an instant and then he nodded again.

"I know what it is. He has no desire to speak with Mr. Grantford," exclaimed Percy.

Oliver wheeled upon him and cried: "You talk too much!"

"Well, dammit, I suggested as much back in the carriage, and you denied it. I still do not consider it sufficient reason why we must fork out double the fare."

"It will not be anything like double. Look you, Percy, you have got it easy, but I have got to be able to argue my case with my father. Well, burn me, if I know what I am going to say to him."

"That you have a wish to marry Miss Sophie Sandringham, the sister of the countess of Dalby."

"And what if he then goes on to demand of me what my bride and I shall be subsisting on? Then what am I to say to him?"

Percy subsided with the remark: "Ah, that is a hard one."

Oliver turned to Lady Dalby. "So you see, my

lady, why I must beg to be relieved of my pledge to Sophie. I am sure the governor will cut me off without a cent."

"Oh, Oliver, I still would marry you!" exclaimed Sophie.

"Now, child, do be sensible," said her ladyship. "Oliver, indeed, has something to worry about. It is not all cakes and ale for him, as it is for Percy." She turned to Oliver and said: "But, Oliver, it is just possible that you are leaping to unwarranted conclusions. You have got to go to your father and lay your case before him. You never can tell, but he might be more than inclined to assist you in some way more than you think. Furthermore, Sophie will not come to you a pauper as I came to *my* husband. His lordship has indicated a willingness to take a hand in the marriage portions of my sisters. That should go some distance with Mr. Grantford, for the earl can afford to be generous, seeing as how it would relieve him of the worry of two mischievous brats," she ended with a chuckle.

"You give me heart, my lady, but my father is a hard-nosed chap and not easily swayed by the usual considerations. He is ambitious for the Grantfords and looks upon me to do my share. Unfortunately, I am damned if I know precisely what he has in mind, except that it may be he intends to have the final say upon every decision in my life. I never seem to be able to satisfy him—even when I try."

"Perhaps if my lord earl invited him to London so that they could have a long chat. Perhaps that might clear up things. Surely whatever it is that your father has in mind for you, connections with the Desfords are hardly to be looked down upon. There is every reason to believe that his lordship will assume the robe of lord chief justice in time. He is quite a brilliant man is my husband."

"If his lordship would be so kind, I should be indebted to him for the rest of my life."

"Then what say you put off your return to Woodhouse and come to dinner tonight, after which we can lay it all before Lord Dalby?" suggested Lady Dalby.

"I am forever at your service, my lady."

"Oh, I say!" exclaimed Percy in a woeful tone. "I do not know how we can do it. The thing is I am going to be running short of funds and we have already given up our rooms, so we haven't a place to stay, not even on tick. Once I pay off the post boy, my pockets will have but a few guineas before they are to let."

"Can you not get any more?" asked Oliver, surprised.

"What, do you think all I have to do is go to the nearest tree and pluck pounds and pence from it? My banking connection is in Loughborough, and I never thought I should have to extend it to London. I have just barely enough to get us back to Woodhouse in reasonable comfort. I fear that we shall have to put the business off for a bit. Perhaps another, later, visit."

Lady Dalby shook her head impatiently. "No, I am sure that that will not be necessary. Leave it to my lord. I am sure he will be able to see you lodged in comfort, and you can settle your expenses with him later. One has got to put first things first, Percy, and you will have to agree that Oliver's business must come before all other considerations."

"As it may please you, my lady," replied Percy.

"In any case, we have got plenty of rooms available in this house, and for tonight, I am sure that we can put you up. Now, do you go and settle with the post boy. You shall not be needing his services for a bit."

Chapter 4

That evening, when Lord Dalby returned from his judicial duties to the peace and comfort of his home, he was put out of countenance to discover that not only had he a pair of lodgers for the night but also that he had been elected locum tenens for Mr. Grantford by a constituency of one, namely Lady Dalby. He took it all in good stride, one look at the anxiety in Sophie's face convincing him that he had no recourse but to give his attention to the matter. He agreed to see the young gentlemen provided for during their extended stay in the city but begged off giving it his immediate attention until some rather harrowing cases currently occupying him could be brought to a conclusion. He had a great deal of studying to do, for a particularly sticky precedent was involved in one of them and he had got some extraordinarily skillful barristers to deal with.

Oliver and Percy were both quite relieved to have their problems postponed in such a pleasant way, for neither of them particularly wanted to part company with his twin. Oliver was especially thankful that the scene with his father would not only now be postponed but might never have to occur.

Naturally, Sarah was quite pleased with the prospect of having Percy close by and immediately began to make plans for going about with him. On the other hand, although she hid her thoughts, inwardly Sophie considered it all a bit of nonsense. She saw no reason for the delay because she could not see how Mr. Grantford could be anything but pleased with the match. She tended to be a little short with Oliver because of this defect in his character but said nothing to the point to him about it. But, from the moment it began to appear that the blessing of her troth to Oliver by Mr. Grantford was to be dclayed for an interminable length of time, she quietly began to make plans of her own, right there at the dinner table.

Since neither of the young Sandringham ladies had ever backed off from a bit of fun for lack of nerve, it stood to reason that the daring scheme she had devised, which should have been a horror of disreputable behavior to a lady of her class, was contemplated without the turning of a hair.

All during dinner, and the conversation period

before retiring for the night which followed, Sophie was rather quiet for a Sandringham twin. Lady Dalby noticed her slight air of abstraction but attributed it to her disappointment with the events that had occurred. She did not think to pass any remark upon it, respecting her sister's privacy in the matter of her anguish.

The ladies retired before the gentlemen but not by much. Lord Dalby had a heavy day in court facing him on the morrow, and the two young gentlemen were quite beat from the physical exertion of travel coupled with the strain they both were under until Oliver's business could be attended to.

The twins had very little to say to each other as they prepared for bed and were in bed in very short order. Sarah contentedly fell asleep rather quickly, but Sophie lay upon her back staring up into the darkness, waiting.

The sounds of the house diminished gradually during the next two hours until stillness reigned throughout. When Sophie was assured that there would be no one to witness her activities, she began to ease herself from under the covers.

Sarah immediately stirred and mumbled: "Are you not asleep yet?" and Sophie gently slid back down, not answering. The steady breathing of her sister resumed, and Sophie waited a little longer just to make sure. Then, ever so much more carefully, without raising the covers, she slid out from under them and quietly began to move about the room, collecting those articles of clothing whose location she had marked in her mind's eye as she had been getting ready for bed. She was very quiet at her labor and forbore to put on her boots until she was fully clothed and standing outside her chamber door. She carried her little bundle of clothing to the head of the stairs where she deposited it and then made her way to the chamber occupied by Percy.

Standing just outside, she placed her ear against his door and listened attentively. She could just make out his snoring and, satisfied that he was deep in slumber, she tried the latch on his door with the greatest of caution. It was well oiled and turned easily and noiselessly. She gave silent thanks to Lord Dalby for the high quality of his servants.

She entered the room, not a little embarrassed. She kept her thoughts away from the likelihood of what might ensue if she were to be discovered in the bedchamber of her sister's fiancé and held purposefully to her task—the locating of the clothing he had been wearing that day. It proved quite easy to find, for apparently no manservant had been assigned to him and his attire lay in rumpled folds over a chair.

It was quite dark in the chamber, only a tiny, shaded light was burning, and she was completely unfamiliar with the strange garments. But she finally located his coat and felt the heavy weight of his wallet, which she quickly extracted. From it she withdrew a packet of notes and put the wallet back on the top of the little pile of disordered clothing. She crept out of the room as silently as she had entered, collected her bundle at the head of the stairs, descended and passed the footman, asleep at his post, as she made her way out into the square.

She never paused until she had got to the opposite side of the street, nor did she even pause to look back, so that she missed a figure, cloaked just as she was, who, as silently, was dogging her footsteps some thirty paces behind her.

She stopped to catch her breath. It seemed to her that she had been holding it ever since she had begun the preparations for her flight, but now that she could rest a bit, she was feeling much better. The hardest part was done. By comparison, the rest of it would be ever so much easier. She was beginning to relax when a voice behind her exclaimed in a sharp whisper: "Sophie! How could you? Why?!"

For a moment she thought it was her own conscience, since it was so very much like her own voice, but her common sense told her otherwise and she turned with a gasp and cried, hoarsely: "Sarah! You followed me!"

"Obviously, sister dear. Now, precisely what are you about? This stealing of my fiancé's money is just like stealing mine, so I suspect that there is something you are about to do with it. Pray, what do you have in mind?"

Sophie tossed her chin and replied: "I am going home to speak with Mr. Grantford. Oliver may be afraid to tackle his father, but I certainly am not, nor am I about to stand on my thumbs while our nice menfolk discuss and debate until the cows come home. Since Percy is about to become my brother-in-law and can rely upon Alan to see him through the loss of his notes, I do not see that he can have the least objection to making a loan to his future sister-in-law. Oliver can pay him back and be happy to do so once I have accomplished what I have set out to do."

"Oh, Sophie, I know exactly how you must be feeling, but this is no proper way to go about it," protested Sarah.

"If you will show me a better, I am prepared to follow it," rejoined Sophie, firmly.

"But be sensible, sister dear. You cannot go traveling about, a lone female. Gentlewomen do not do these things; no, not even in Leicestershire."

"I cannot help it. This gentlewoman intends to do just so. Now, do you return to the house, and I pray you will not arouse them until the morning. I must have my chance, love."

"Well, I am not about to allow you to go all by yourself. How much money did you pilfer from Percy?"

"I have not the slightest idea. He said, before dinner, that there was enough to see Oliver and himself back to Leicestershire in comfort. I relied upon his word."

"Well, in that case, why are we standing about? Let us get on with it. How do you intend to proceed?" said Sarah, smiling.

Sophie positively giggled in her joy and relief at having her sister and her dearest friend for company on what could prove to be a most troublesome business. It made it more like old times, something of a lark that their arriving at mature womanhood threatened to bring to an end forever.

"We have got to locate the Bull and Mouth Inn, for there is where we can find a post chaise to take us home. I heard the boys say that that is where they hired their rig—but, Sarah, you have got nothing to wear! You will need at least one complete change."

"Well, if you had only let me in on it, I could have come all prepared. Now we needs must return to the house so that I can collect a few things."

"Oh, no, Sarah, you would not rouse the house against me, would you?"

"Well, of course, I would not!" exclaimed Sarah in high dudgeon. "Against my own sister? Would you do as much if you were in my shoes?"

Sophie reached for her hand and squeezed it lovingly. "Very well. If we have done it once, I am sure we can do it again—but quietly."

They started to stroll back across the square. Suddenly Sophie exclaimed: "Oh, dear, how shall we go about it? I mean to say one female traveling by herself is bad enough, but two gentlewomen without attendants must be the subject of much notice."

"Yes, we shall have to do something about that. But it could be quite easily done, I think. There would be nothing exceptional in a gentlewoman traveling with her companion, now, would there?"

"Why, yes, that might do it— Oh, but no! That

is never for us! We can never be mistaken for anything but what we are—sisters!"

Sarah sighed in disappointment. "Yes, I had forgot. Well, what do *you* suggest?"

Sophie pondered for a moment, and then she stopped. "Yes, that is it! An abigail!"

"Now, where in heaven's name are we to find an abigail at this time of night—not to say that we have not sufficient funds for one?"

"No, no, *you* can be the abigail!"

"But that is nonsense! No one will ever believe that a mistress and her abigail could have the same face!"

"I will wear a veil."

"Do we have one?"

"No-o—but I am sure we can fashion one from one of our lace bibs."

"Well, I do not see that we need an abigail, then. I can go along as your hired companion."

"No, I think an abigail will make me more unapproachable. It will look much better, I am sure, a lady traveling with her abigail."

"Yes, I am forced to agree. Makes it all more respectable somehow—but I am not so sure I shall like having to fetch and carry for you all that great trip."

"Silly! You will not have to. We can take turns, don't you see. What are we twins for?"

Sarah laughed. "But of course! I say, Sophie, I must be getting rusty. I think we shall have to do this sort of thing more often or we shall be in danger of losing our art."

*   *   *

The girls, past masters at the art of entering their residence by stealth, eased themselves back into the house, tiptoed upstairs to their room and gathered all that was needed for their forthcoming travels. It did not take them very long, and they were out of the house and back in the square in less than twenty minutes. The skies to the east were beginning to show the first faint signs of the new day, and they quickly decamped from Cavendish Square, gaining the greatest confidence from the ease with which they had managed thus far.

All they had to go on was their knowledge that the Bull and Mouth was within an easy walk of the Temple and the Temple was quite on the other side of the city, close to the Thames. Since they had not the vaguest idea where the waterfront was from Cavendish Square, they chose a direction and proceeded along it, hoping to find a very late cabbie—or a very early one, whatever the case might be—who would carry them to their destination.

It was just as well for them that they did, for the banks of the Thames at that hour were overrun with riffraff and worse and no place at all for a gentlewoman to find herself at any time.

London was just beginning to come alive, and so they had not very far to walk before they came upon a hackney carriage, with its horse and driver dozing in the growing light. They woke him up without ceremony and with such an imperious manner that the poor man had no time to wonder what a veiled lady and her abigail were doing out upon

London's streets at such an ungodly hour. He took them to the Bull and Mouth, receiving his fare with no great enthusiasm, and went off to find a more quiet spot to finish his interrupted slumbers. The horse must have been in the same case as its master, for by the time its lethargic exertions brought the girls to the hostelry, dawn was definitely coming up.

They went inside and inquired about posting to Loughborough in Leicestershire. They had reason to bless Percy, for his remark anent the current state of his pocket proved quite accurate, even to the extra miles necessary to carry them to Woodhouse. They proceeded to have breakfast and were served with every attention. Posting such a distance called for more resources than even fairly affluent travelers could afford. In a little while, quite refreshed and brimming with exultant confidence, the young ladies found themselves ensconced in a post chaise threading its way out of London on the North Road.

Chapter 5

On this particular morning, the new day of the Desford household in Cavendish Square started pretty much as the days before it. The countess, who had had some qualms about all that must face her as she came into her new station in life, had managed to fill her position with a great competence, unusual in a lady of the lower gentry. Perhaps it was that her husband, also quite new to his title, was not as demanding and quite content with anything that she could devise, since he had been a bachelor who was bound to find any version of domesticity a vast improvement over his former single state. In any case, the household did run well, and this day was no exception until an excited upstairs maid came bursting into the breakfast room, followed by a perturbed Jepperson, the butler.

His lordship looked up from his morning journal but left it to his countess to speak.

"Yes, Jepperson, is something amiss?" she asked.

"Indeed, your ladyship, I fear so. It is the young ladies—they are nowhere to be found."

"Oh, I dare say they have gone out with their young men for a morning stroll about the square. I am sure they will be back before long, for they have not had their breakfast."

"No, madam, I fear it is worse than that. I have looked in on the young gentlemen, and they are just now in the process of preparing to come down. I thought it best not to make inquiry of them."

The earl was frowning now. "Do you say that their beds have not been slept in?"

"No, my lord. Nora here says that they have been, but some of their clothing is gone with them."

"Missing?"

"I fear so, my lord."

"Now, what in blazes can they be up to? Pennie, what do you think?"

Lady Dalby was frowning. "It is decidedly odd. I cannot think of anything that they could be up to. No, I am sure that they have gone out early to visit Aunt Claudia. They have not seen the dear soul since they stayed with her those few weeks. Indeed, that must be it. I am sure of it."

Oliver and Percy came in just then, looking well rested and quite spruce, but there was a look of concern on their faces, and Percy had his wallet in his hand.

Lady Dalby, observing their troubled countenances, immediately asked: "So you have heard? What do you know of it?"

Both of them were a bit startled, and Percy waved his wallet saying: "Just this, my lady. Er—would you be kind enough to dismiss the servants? It is most embarrassing that anything of the sort should have occurred in the Desford residence."

"I do not see how that will help," remarked the earl. "What the devil does your wallet have to do with it?"

"I do think it would be ever so much better if I did not have to make any accusations before the servants, my lord."

"You say the servants are involved? By heaven, I shall send to Bow Street at once! Jepperson, go immediately to—"

"Just a moment, my lord," Lady Dalby intervened. "I think it would be far wiser for us to learn all we can before the police are called in, don't you?" She turned to Percy. "Is it kidnapping for ransom you suspect? Oh, dear God, I do hope that it is not so!"

"Kidnapping? Heavens, no!" exclaimed Percy. "It is merely that someone has filched the notes out of my wallet. I mean to say now, we cannot have that in so respectable a house as this, can we?"

"What *are* you talking about?" demanded the earl. "We are speaking of the twins. Have you seen them?"

Percy drew himself up, and Oliver's face darkened as Percy exclaimed: "My lord, I should never for one moment ever make such a charge against either Sarah or Sophie. How could you ever think I would? Why, it must be one of the servants, I am sure."

His lordship turned to Lady Dalby and asked: "My sweet, can you make head or tail of this conversation? I have the distinct feeling that we are not speaking to the same point at all."

"I know what you mean, Alan. I feel a bit lost myself. Percy, pray tell us precisely what this filching has to do with the twins?"

"Not a thing!" he replied, staunchly. "I never said it did!"

"But then, where are they? Do you have any knowledge of their whereabouts at this moment?"

"But I assure you, my lady, neither Sarah nor Sophie could possibly be involved. I never said they were."

The earl brought his fist crashing down upon the tabletop. "Silence!" he thundered. "Percy and Oliver, do you or do you not know where my sisters-in-law are at this very moment?"

Percy gulped. "No, your lordship."

Oliver shook his head and asked: "Don't you know, my lord?"

"No, I do not, and that is precisely what we are trying to find out. Now pray tell me what is all this nonsense about your wallet?"

"It is empty, my lord," replied Percy, holding it open for all to see.

"Is there something unusual in that condition?"

"I had upward of forty pounds in it, last night. Of that I am certain. I had enough to make a trip back to Leicestershire with Oliver by post chaise. If you will recall, my lady, I said as much yesterday, and you were kind enough to offer your hospitality so that we could stay on and discuss Oliver's troubles with his lordship."

Lady Dalby frowned. "Yes, I do recall that, and it strikes me that, somehow, there is a connection in it." She turned to the earl. "Alan, do you see if the girls took one of our vehicles while I question Nora, here, and then I shall go up and inspect their room. Jepperson, pray send someone out to my aunt, Miss Dampier, on the chance that Miss Sophie and Miss Sarah have gone to pay her a visit. It is not so great a stroll, and they do not stand upon ceremony with my aunt."

The feeling of helplessness that had pervaded the breakfast room vanished as everyone began to find something to do in regard to this mysterious disappearance. Oliver and Percy busied themselves with a room by room search of the premises, looking for anything that might suggest an explanation, but hoping that they would find their loves in some remote corner, engaged in some prank.

An hour later, the earl, Lady Dalby, Oliver and Percy were assembled in the sitting room off the grand parlor. Their expressions attested to more than their failure to learn anything further regarding the girls. In their minds now lurked a suspicion of foul play, and they were hesitant to say so, putting it off lest it prove to be true.

They sat grimly together. The earl was frowning and shaking his head; Oliver looked frightened and Percy, confused and worried. But Lady Dalby was staring hard at the wall, lost in thought.

Finally, Lord Dalby stood up with an air of resignation. "There is nothing for it, my love, but to call in the runners. We cannot sit and do nothing."

But her ladyship remained lost in thought and did not respond. His lordship raised his hand to the bellrope, and that brought her ladyship's hand up in an arresting gesture.

"No, Alan, not just yet. There is something here that I have on the tip of my tongue to say—but I just do not see the connection."

His lordship lowered his hand and waited. Oliver and Percy stared at Lady Dalby, hope beginning to light up in their eyes.

"It is the connection that baffles me. I am sure there *is* the connection."

"My dear, perhaps if you were to explain your thinking to us at this point, we might see what it is that is the problem."

"Well, Alan, I have been upstairs to speak with the maids and I have the feeling there is no thief amongst them. If we assume, for the moment, that that is true, then there is a connection between the disappearance of the girls and the disappearance of Percy's money. They do seem to have disappeared at about the same time. What is more, there is nothing else taken except for four outfits of the girls'. That would be two apiece. Do you see what I am beginning to get at?"

Lord Dalby frowned and shook his head. "No, for it sounds as though they were going on a trip."

"Precisely so. A trip. Oh, but you truly are clever, Alan!"

"But where the deuce would they want to go to?"

"Well, now, that is where the wallet comes in, don't you see?"

"Not at all."

"Percy said before the girls and me that he had just enough funds to take himself and Oliver back home. If the girls had any reason to want to go home, it was like offering them a ticket to travel."

Oliver demanded: "But why should they want to go home? Percy and I are here."

Lady Dalby threw up her hands in despair. "That is as far as I have gotten. I do not see what connection there is between their wish to go home and anything else—but I am almost convinced that it is they who are up to something and that no foul play is involved."

Percy stood up and folded his arms across his chest, looking quite noble. "Nothing can make me believe that my love would stoop so low as to steal from me."

At which Lady Dalby laughed and retorted: "Then I suggest, and strongly, Mr. Deverill, that you had better get acquainted with your love."

Percy, discomfited, sat back down.

The earl was chuckling. "Methinks that I had best secure my wallet under my pillow at nights."

"Do you really think that would prove any sort of protection, O my lord and master?"

His lordship laughed, and the faces of Oliver and Percy went rosy red.

"You should be ashamed of yourself, my lady," chided the earl, grinning. "You forget we have tender ears present."

Her ladyship laughed and tendered her apologies to the gentlemen, which only deepened the color on their cheeks despite their grins.

Then Lady Dalby's face grew sober and she said: "But, Alan, what are we to do?"

"Are you so very sure that Leicestershire is where they went off to?"

"I cannot think that they would have run off to any other place. After all, they are sensible girls."

"My lady, I pray you will pardon me if I take some exception to your statement. But seriously speaking, I do not think that it is anything to worry about. Of course, we shall have to send after them because I should hate to think what trouble they would manage to find for themselves all alone in Woodhouse. Truly I am inclined to agree that that is where they are headed, and it should not be so difficult to come up with them if one were to start right off. As things stand, I am forced to remain in London because of my official duties but—"

"I shall go after them!" declared Oliver. "It is my right!"

"And that is my fiancée, too! So it is my right as well!"

"And pray what will you do with them once you

have caught up with them, pray tell?" asked the earl. "By the time you do reach them, starting so late as this, you will be in the Banbury neighborhood, I should surmise—that is, if it is by post chaise they have gone. If they caught the stage, they will reach Woodhouse before you ever could."

"Not my sisters, my lord. I can assure you they will have traveled by post chaise," said Lady Dalby.

"Ye-es, I am sure of it," drawled his lordship. "My dear, in any event I do not think it wise that the dears be allowed to roam about Leicestershire unchaperoned. I venture to say the county is but just recovering from having had to suffer them for all these past years. I am sure our dear neighbors back home could never survive a second invasion. Much as the necessity brings pain to my heart, my lady, I fear you must accompany these two in their travels so that you can bring your authority to bear upon your sisters when you find them."

"Thank you, Alan. I am relieved that you see the necessity for my leaving you. Needless to say, my sisters are bound to have a warm time of it when I do get up with them."

"I am sure of it. And I pray you will not neglect to add a word or two or three in my behalf as well."

Chapter 6

It happened on the road, between Bragenham and Stoke Hammond. The post boy had seen the small but deep rut in the road and had maneuvered the chaise to avoid catching his wheels in it, but one of the rear wheels came too close and slipped into it. Expert driver that he was, the post boy, instantly realizing what had happened, brought his team to a stop so quickly that the leaders reared high in the air as the strong pull on the reins forced them to fight the air to maintain their balance. The feel of the vehicle was changed, and the post boy did not dare to proceed until he had ascertained the extent of any damage that the carriage had sustained.

Holding onto the reins, he stepped down, soothing the horses all the while, and, when they were quieted down, began an inspection of the chaise's underpinnings. He discovered that the rear wheel had not come through its ordeal unscathed. In fact it was a miracle that it still held its end of the carriage up. Only the iron tire was holding it together, for all the spokes showed signs of cracks, and the wheel was out of round and no longer trued up to the axle. A few more feet of travel and it would have come to pieces, dropping the body down onto the road in a most catastrophic manner. It was obvious that they could not proceed until the axle was inspected by a competent wheelwright and a new wheel fitted to the vehicle.

He stepped to the window of the chaise and informed the lady and her abigail of their misfortune in a most regretful manner, assuring them that he had done his level best to avoid the accident even as he silently prayed that the gratuity he had expected for providing safe and speedy transportation had not been completely jeopardized. As it was, he knew he would have the devil's own time of it with the master of the posting, getting repaid for whatever he would have to lay out in repairs. He was something less than happy.

The situation for the ladies was not a pleasant one, and it needed no discussion between them to make it clearer. The post boy laid out the facts of their predicament and they had no choice but to accept his decisions.

Neither Bragenham nor Stoke Hammond were sufficiently great places to support a wheelwright.

He would have to go five miles back to Linslade to find an expert mechanic and, as it was unlikely that the fellow's shop would chance to have in its stock a new wheel to fit the chaise, one would have to be fashioned and fitted. This would necessitate some sort of jury rig to tow the incapacitated vehicle back to the shop where it could be worked on. In short, they could not count upon continuing their journey in the chaise if they could not afford to lose a day or two. If it was their pleasure, he could arrange to secure another post vehicle from the local innkeeper so that they would not be inconvenienced, and he could retrieve his own chaise on his return—but, of course, as he had not the funds to accomplish the transfer, he was forced to rely on the lady's pocketbook to bridge the gap, as it were.

The veiled lady requested him to move out of earshot so that she could consult with her maid. When he was gone away, Sarah lifted up her veil and said to Sophie: "Well, isn't this a fine how-de-do! Heaven only knows for how long I shall be stuck with having to wear the veil! One can hardly breathe in the awful thing. The next time we do this, we have got to have a proper veil made out of very light stuff."

Replied Sophie: "Oh, Sarah, I am so sorry, but who could have expected it? If it is so distressing, and I know how it can be, we can change back right now. The fellow cannot see us, I do not think."

"No, no, it is all right. We have not the time, for we have got to think. We have not sufficient funds to take advantage of his suggestion, yet we cannot linger about this district for so long. I truly do not have a clue as to what we are going to do, but of this I am certain, we shall have to lose time no matter what."

"I dare say, but we have got to come to the point. We have got to do something right at this moment. As long as we sit here and he lolls about waiting for us to say something, time is wasting. I think we should send him on his way."

"Yes, you are right—but two females at the side of the road in a disabled carriage—well, I mean to say we could be subject to all manner of indignities before he ever gets back to us."

Sophie shrugged. "I fear we have no choice. We shall just have to endure it. We can close up the windows and draw the blinds so that it looks as though there is no one in it, and perhaps, passersby will not be too inquisitive."

"It is hardly to be preferred, but I do not see that we have any choice. Call the fellow back."

Further conference with the post boy resulted in his unhitching the team and hobbling three of the horses in a nearby field. He resumed his saddle on the leader, which was his usual place as driver of a post chaise, and sped off back to Linslade.

The ladies shut up the windows and drew down the blinds. In the murky atmosphere of the closed-up chaise, they sat back on the squabs to wait.

"Have you any idea how far we have come?" asked Sarah, patting her cheeks, which were damp from perspiration.

"Sarah, we can change places now that we are alone, if you would like."

"No, we dare not risk it. I can hear carriages on the road. You can never tell when some Paul Pry must have a go at satisfying his bone of curiosity. I say, it must be approaching the noon hour."

"So late as that? Oh, I hope not. Surely we have not been traveling so long. Why, we are but come to Buckinghamshire."

"Well, you were no help at all upon that score, my dear. Look you, Sophie, it seems to me you are being quite sweet to the fellow and I am sure he has not his mind on the journey."

"Well, you will admit it all has gone to make the trip a deal more easy. Did you not see how he fell all over his shoes to fetch us cool water at the last change? I think I know quite well how to play the role of abigail to a lady."

Sophie went on: "Well, I pray he will not tarry now. The sooner we can get back to Linslade, the sooner we shall know just how badly off we are. It might be better than he thought. If I understood him correctly, if the wheelwright should happen to have a suitable wheel in his shop, we might be on our way in just a matter of hours instead of days. Oh, I do hope so! I am sure that by this time, Pennie will have figured out something and sent people after us. Sarah, you know how important it is to me to get to Woodhouse before anyone can interfere!"

"Have you given any thought to what you will say to Mr. Grantford?"

Sophie shrugged and sighed. "It is awfully diffi-

cult to think of anything. I mean to say it is not exactly the office of the bride-to-be to ask for the
hand of her groom from his father, is it?"

"I suspect that you will have the advantage of
surprise at least," said Sarah with a chuckle. "It is
the last thing that a father can expect. Do you
know if Oliver has even hinted of his engagement
to you to his father?"

"Knowing Oliver's penchant for correspondence,
I wonder if his father even knows where he is."

Sarah chuckled. "In that case, I dare say it will
be something more than a surprise to Mr. Grantford."

"More than shock, I am sure. Actually it might
turn out to be quite funny. Oh, dear, I do hope that
my future father-in-law has a sense of humor. It
would be the most difficult thing to go through the
business in the face of a dour countenance."

"Have no fear, pet. I shall be at your right hand
to give you heart."

"Not on my life! It is something I must do for
myself. Sarah, you must promise that you will not
interfere and, knowing you as well as I know myself, you can not come with me or you could not
resist having your say in the business. I shall have
my fill of worry with the 'governor,' as Oliver refers
to him, without having the added burden of a
saucy, loquacious sister. In any case, we certainly
do not wish to confuse Mr. Grantford with a pair of
look-alikes at so important an occasion."

"Oh, I do not know. I think it might add so
much more fun to the scene."

"Sarah Sandringham!"

"All right, Sophie, have it as you will. I promise not to be present—but you must promise that you will relate to me everything that was said between you afterward."

"Well, you know I shall. Tell me, what time do you think I should plan to see Mr. Grantford?"

"When you get there, of course."

"No, no! I mean to say early or late?"

"What do you mean?"

"Well, you know how men are. Some are so grouchy if they are come upon when they have appointed the hour for some particular purpose."

"My dear, considering *your* purpose, I do not think it will make the slightest difference. Mr. Grantford is in for a shock whatever the hour."

Sophie looked glum as she nodded. "I begin to think that it may not be the wisest thing to do at any hour."

"Well, I should think that having come this far, you have just got to go through with it or make us out to be a pair of foolish females."

"You really ought to have stopped me, you know."

"I am sure I did try, but you were quite set upon doing it. In any case, it *is* a bit of a lark. I was beginning to get bored with London's idea of entertainment. All it is is one crush upon another. There are just too many people running about loose. Once I am wed I am sure it will be quite different. Then I shan't be pushed into trying to go everywhere and visit everybody at once."

"Well, I shall not be unhappy to give London up completely. Give me the peace and quiet of our Leicestershire hills. Is it not fortunate that Oliver need not stay in the city?"

"Oh, I shan't envy you—in any case, Percy and I can always take a holiday and come up to Beaumanor. I am sure Alan would allow it."

"I shall not be happy to be so far from you."

"Nor I from you, sweet sister."

There was a moist look in their eyes for a bit and they were silent.

Suddenly Sophie sat up and said: "Hark! Is that the post boy returned?"

There was a knocking on the door of the chaise and a voice called out: "I say, is someone within? Is anybody hurt in there? Do you require assistance?"

"Shhh!" whispered Sarah. "Perhaps he will go away."

"Put up your veil just in case!"

Sarah arranged the veil, and both girls held their breath.

"Damnation!" muttered the voice. "This could be quite serious. I had better have a look to be sure."

The door came open, and the glare of daylight quite blinded the girls as they shrank back. They could only make out a huge dark shape blocking the opening.

But there was no menace at all in the quiet voice that said: "I beg your pardon, ladies, but I could not pass by without making certain that my aid was not required. I could see that the chaise must have had a bit of a jolt. Are you ladies in any distress?"

Sarah, as the lady, responded: "I thank you, good sir, for your concern, but there is no need to put yourself to any trouble. Our driver is returning shortly with aid for the vehicle and we are quite unharmed."

Although the stranger was paying heed to her, his eyes were staring at Sophie; his face being in the shadow, no other details of his features could be discerned. From his diction and his manner, though, it was obvious that he was, at least, a gentleman.

The girls felt a little more at ease and slowly sat up as they tried hard to make out his face. He seemed to realize their difficulty and stepped a little back so that the sunlight lit up his face.

It was an interesting physiognomy. They could see that his hair was thick and black, falling over a broad brow. His eyebrows were dark and appeared even heavier than they were, for his eyes were deep-set and brooding, even though he was smiling softly at them. The rest of his face was clean cut and nothing extraordinary, giving an unexceptional appearance. He could not have been past his thirty-fifth year.

"I am John Linscombe and I reside at Linscombe Park, just over the rise but some two miles by road from this spot. It appears to me that you ladies are in need of refreshment, if not some rest, after your experience. I should be delighted if it would please you to take advantage of my house to restore yourselves."

Sarah replied: "Indeed, good sir, you are too kind. I am sure you must realize that appearances conspire to forbid us to take advantage of your invitation—oh, I beg your pardon— What is it, Sophie?"

Sophie had been tugging at her sleeve. "Oh, Miss Sandringham, surely it cannot hurt anything to accept the gentleman's invitation. After all, I am your chaperone."

Sarah peered through her veil at her sister as Mr. Linscombe said: "I pray, madam, that you will heed your maid. I can assure you there is nothing improper, implied or intended. My mother resides with me and will make you welcome for my sake, if for no other."

To his great surprise, he saw the veiled lady join hands with her maid and say: "Do you think we may, Sophie?"—his shock being augmented to hear the maid respond: "Oh, Sarah, let us do it!"

"But what of the post boy? He is bound to return soon with the wheelwright."

Mr. Linscombe, recovering himself quickly, suggested: "I shall be pleased to have my man come to stand guard by the chaise, and if he should miss your driver, he can go on into Linslade and relay any instructions you may wish to send to your driver. There are only two wheelwrights in town, and he is bound to find the post boy at one of them—or did your man go on to Bletchley?"

"No, it was to Linslade he returned. Well, Mr. Linscombe, in that case, I am sure that we can have no further objection. We should be most grateful for your hospitality," replied Sarah.

But Mr. Linscombe was not heeding her this time. He stood enthralled as he bathed in the brilliant warm smile conferred upon him by the lovely lady's-maid.

Chapter 7

Mr. Linscombe's vehicle proved to be a less than modest dogcart, that so very useful and unstylish vehicle used for just about every purpose of transportation on estates and farms both large and small. The girls could see at a glance that the beast harnessed to the utilitarian vehicle was no ordinary beast of burden. Although standing docilely by the side of the road, the gelding's lines spoke of power and endurance, the sort of animal much in demand in Leicestershire Chase country. It was obvious that the animal was worth a yardful of the vehicle he was hitched to.

"I say, you must excuse the dogcart. Had I known I would encounter such lovely ladies in need, I would have brought along the family state coach."

He paused uncertainly before the dogcart and then he shrugged his shoulders. Turning to Sarah, he said: "I am sure that the lady would prefer to sit beside the driver rather than stare back at the road in a rear seat."

Sarah nodded and prepared to ascend up to the seat when she was brushed aside by Sophie, who turned and stared at her intensely. Sarah backed off with a frown and said: "Mr. Linscombe, I am sure that I should prefer the rear seat if you have no objection."

Mr. Linscombe was blinking in surprise. It was unheard of that a lady should yield the more desirable seat to her maid. But not one to question Dame Fortune when she was in a mood to bless him, he quickly moved to see her seated while he assured her that the road to his home was quite smooth, the horse was gentle and they should be traveling at an easy pace. Sarah merely nodded, her smile behind the veil, of course, could not be seen. Riding on the rear seat of a dogcart was nothing new to her.

Then Mr. Linscombe gave his attention to the maid, helping her up to a seat beside himself with a pleasure that shone in his eyes. He was rewarded with a smile that quite made his day—if the previous one had not.

He held the reins still for a moment and turned his head to address the lady: "Madam, are you—?"

Sarah interrupted him with: "Mr. Linscombe, perhaps it would be better if I introduced myself, since there is no one about to do the office. I am Miss Sandringham, and that is my maid, Sophie."

"I am indebted to you, Miss Sandringham. Now, if you are quite comfortable, we shall be off."

"Please."

He urged up the horse and they started off at a leisurely pace.

"You ladies were headed north," he said as they rolled along. "May I inquire as to your destination?"

Again he was surprised, but overjoyed, when it was the maid beside him who responded.

"We are going home to Beaumanor, an estate near Woodhouse in Leicestershire."

"Ah, I do believe I have heard of the place. The 'hunting earl,' as I have heard. Dalby, isn't it? Always had a wish to join in the hunt up there, but I have no acquaintances in that district. Are you related to this earl, perhaps? That is, I mean is your mistress some relation of his?"

"Er—we have a connection in that direction, but Lord Harry Desford, whom you are referring to, has died since, and there is a new earl."

"I see. How very interesting. I think I should like to gain an acquaintanceship with this new chap."

"Oh, that is easily arranged. I am sure that Alan—er, my sis—oh, my mistress could see to it," said Sophie, blushing furiously in her confusion. It had never been a part of the plan to carry their masquerade so far.

"Sophie, if that is your wish, I should be delighted to speak to my brother-in-law, the earl of Dalby, in Mr. Linscombe's behalf," said Sarah from behind, and there was an unmistakable note of mirth in her tone.

"Miss Sandringham, I will thank you to mind your own business!" snapped Sophie.

Mr. Linscombe gasped and involuntarily jerked the reins, so that the horse lost its footing for a moment.

It brought Sophie to a realization of how far out of character she had strayed, and she immediately tried to patch it up. "Oh, madam, I beg you will forgive me my outburst. I promise I shall never so forget my place again," she declared in woeful tones.

"You had better make sure, girl, or it is the sack for you. I am sure I can easily find ten better maids than you have been to me," rejoined Sarah.

"Oh, I would not think of contradicting you, Miss Sandringham."

"Sophie, are you forgetting your appointment in Woodhouse?" asked Sarah, all curiosity.

"I am sure that Miss Sandringham will grant that that is my business and no one else's."

"I just thought I would ask, my dear. Now, do you leave me in peace to enjoy the drive."

Mr. Linscombe's puzzlement had now grown so great that he had to remark. "Miss Sophie, the arrangement between you and your mistress is not in the usual way, I must say."

"No, it is not. Actually, one might say I was more of a companion to her."

"Ah, perhaps that explains it. I was sure that I sensed an undercurrent of levity in your recent exchange—as though her threat was of no consequence."

"Indeed, Mr. Linscombe, you are most observing."

"Are you out from London?"

"Yes. We just left it this morning."

"I say, you have not got very far, have you?"

"Well, of course, if the chaise had not broken down. . . ."

"Yes, of course. I say, have you spent much time in the country? I can tell from your speech that you are not from London originally, nor south of the city."

"Leicestershire is my home."

"Then country living is not a novelty to you. I dare say it is the great city that pleases you most."

"Oh, no, not at all. There are just too, too many parties and not much else."

"Ah, I see. I imagine it is all work and no play for all the time that your mistress is attending balls and things. I should imagine it is enough to make you envious."

Sophie bit her lip to prevent a retort that she knew was not in the character of a maid. Instead she said: "I like a party every now and again, but the life in London is not appealing, for that is all they seem to have. Now, Beaumanor and Charley Forest is a much better life, I think."

"Charley Forest?"

"That is Charnwood Forest. It is still quite a wild place and charming."

"Indeed, I have heard of it. I should very much like to visit it one day."

"Oh, I wish you could! I could show you all the places that I played—oh, I beg your pardon, Mr. Linscombe! I am forgetting my place again," she said with a little smile.

"I do not mind. Please, you were saying?"

Sarah, under her veil, listened to all that was going on behind her and frowned. It was certainly peculiar behavior on Sophie's part to say the least and, as she could not see her sister's expression, she could not know if Sophie was preparing some great jest for the poor gentleman's benefit. She hoped not, for they had trouble enough without further complications. Even going to this chap's home was not going to make things any easier for them. Unless they could speed matters up, Pennie would be in Woodhouse to greet them, and then nothing would get accomplished. Anyway, she was experiencing a wish to be with Percy in the worst way. They had so many things to discuss, and she wanted to talk to Alan about her fiancé's prospects, more because she wanted to hear Lord Dalby praise Percy than for any other reason. She was growing so proud of him.

They had been off the high road for some time and now had come to a fork in this lesser thoroughfare.

As Mr. Linscombe directed the horse up one tine of the fork, he said: "It makes little difference which you take. They both pass a road into Linscombe Park. We are actually driving along the boundary of the place even now."

Sophie merely nodded and Mr. Linscombe seemed a little disappointed. It was rather a large estate and it was very well kept.

"I dare say it is almost as large as Beaumanor," said Sophie, as though in answer to his bafflement.

They came to a great gate and turned in. It was some time before the great house could be seen, and like so many country mansions, it had been constructed in spurts over the centuries, so that one could see all styles of architecture in its various wings and sections. Beaumanor, of only a hundred or so years of age, was a jewel by comparison. Sophie had no comment to make, and Mr. Linscombe experienced further disappointment, not to say how much his puzzlement was increased.

There were a great many workers on the grounds, and buildings and paddocks behind the great house could be seen as the road turned a bit every now and then.

Coming up to the front portal, Mr. Linscombe drew the dogcart to a halt and helped the ladies dismount. Very deliberately, he helped Sophie down first, then proceeded to Miss Sandringham. As he had suspected, she did not seem to mind at all. The puzzle in his mind grew.

He led them into the house and brought them to a sunny room in which an elderly dame was seated, reading a book, while two cats lay at their ease, luxuriating in a sunbeam shining through the window.

"Mother, see what I have brought you! New company for a time!"

She looked at her son with a smile, raising an eyebrow in inquiry, as she gazed at the two young ladies. Her eyes took in the veil and clouded a little. Then they came to rest on Sophie's face and they lighted up a little.

He went on. "I have the pleasure of presenting Miss Sandringham of London and her maid, Miss Sophie."

Mr. Linscombe's mother's face took on a quizzical expression, and she rested her eyes on Sophie once more. Then she looked at her son, waiting.

"Their chaise ran into a spot of trouble, and I offered the hospitality of Linscombe while they waited for repairs. You do not mind?"

"No, I do not mind," she replied, smiling at the ladies as she reached for a bellrope and gave it a tug or two.

A maid responded and was instructed to show the ladies to a spare bedchamber so that they might refresh themselves. Sarah thanked her for her kindness and followed the maid out with Sophie by her side. They were holding each other's hand as they passed from sight.

"Well, my lord, I think there is something strange here," remarked the lady to Mr. Linscombe.

"I never thought you were slow in the attic. Yes, what do you make of it?"

"For the moment, my son, I am not all that interested in the mystery surrounding these young ladies as I am in the mystery that surrounds my son. It can hardly be Miss Sandringham that has moved you to offer the hospitality of our house. She is so thoroughly covered up, I must assume it is the maid that has wakened your interest."

"I'll not deny it. Is she not lovely?"

"But a lady's-maid? Precisely what do you have in mind?"

"It is too early to say—but, if Fortune smiles upon me, their chaise will be a long time in getting itself repaired. Now, then, what do you make of them? Did you notice how close they are? Not the usual distance between a lady and her maid, wouldn't you say?"

"Yes, I would. Either she is no lady's-maid or her mistress is no lady—but, John, I have never known you to entertain strays before."

"I came across the chaise on the high road. It had a badly damaged rear wheel and I investigated it. It was the young lady's face, when I opened the door. A most appealing picture. Rather took to her right away. Thought you would not mind the company for a bit."

"Still, John, it is just not like you. It has been years since any female stirred you even to smile at her. Now, all of a sudden, it is a lady's-maid."

"Perhaps if there were more females about like yon lady's-maid, I would have smiled sooner. She has an air that Martha had."

"Well, I do not see anything of the sort in her. Martha was a lady. Oh, John, do not tell me that you are already in her pocket and you have known her but a few minutes."

He shrugged. "Perhaps—what difference does it

make? She is here and I like the idea. I pray you will be nice to her."

"Well, the pair of them do interest me immensely, I will admit. In any case, I bid you go cautiously. Obviously she is not Martha and not like to make a proper Countess Leighton."

John frowned. "Indeed, but you are perceptive, my lady mother. I certainly intend to see as much of her as I can. My widowerhood suddenly grows overburdensome upon me."

"There are other more eligible fish in the sea, my son. I mean to say you are free to make any arrangement with the girl that you wish. You are certainly old enough—but marriage? A countess has got to fit her station. Do you actually see that young thing as chatelaine of the Linscombes?"

"My lady, do not rush the business. I am very much attracted to the girl is all that I am actually saying at the moment. Give it a chance. We both of us shall have a decent opportunity to see what she is, after a bit. For the moment, you will have to admit, she is no lady's-maid and never was one."

The dowager raised her hand in acceptance. "Very well—and all I am saying is be careful. We shall discuss the matter further after we have had a chance to get better acquainted with the—er—miss."

Lord Leighton smiled. "Thank you, my lady. That is all I would ask of you. Now I must go to the stables and see about sending someone to see to the chaise. I assure you it will not be repaired until I am ready—unless, of course there is some desperate need for it. We shall soon learn. I shall be back shortly."

Sophie came wandering into the sunny little parlor and dipped in curtsy to the older woman. She looked about and finally asked, in disappointed tones: "I beg your pardon, madam, but Mr. Linscombe—is he about?"

Her ladyship smiled and said: "He will return shortly. He has gone to see about sending a man to look after your chaise. Does it belong to Miss Sandringham?"

"Oh no, madam, it is on hire. We are posting up to Leicestershire. I beg your pardon, but Miss Sandringham could not help remarking all the crests about the house. Is there an earl about?"

"Are you familiar with the device of an earl, my girl?"

"Oh, yes, I have seen that of the earl of Dalby, but he is new to the game and has not got it spread about on everything. Then there is an earl of Linscombe?"

"It is my son, the earl of Leighton."

For a moment Sophie stared at the countess, not quite comprehending what she had just been told. Then her cheeks reddened in embarrassment as she dipped into a deep curtsy.

"Oh, I do beg your pardon, my lady. I had no idea!"

"And pray what is your name, my dear?"

"Sand— Oh, you mean *my* name, my lady?"

"Yes, my dear. Sophie what?"

"Yes, my lady. Er—Grantford. Sophie Grantford."

"You are quite sure?"

"Well, of course, my lady. Surely I know my own name," she said rather saucily.

"For a moment there, you did not seem to be so sure, and I had my doubts just as I doubt very much that you are a lady's-maid or, for that matter, any sort of serving-girl at all."

"Oh, but I am, my lady! I assure you that I am."

"Then do you think it proper for a servant to address a countess by other than 'your ladyship'?"

"Oh!" gasped Sophie, her wits completely scattered.

"And, furthermore, young lady, it is something of a surprise to witness a lady holding hands with her abigail as you and Miss Sandringham did before as you left the room."

"Oh, bless me!" exclaimed Sophie, and then she quickly went on to say: "Oh, it is quite all right, your ladyship. It is just that I am not precisely what might be called an abigail. Actually, I am more of a paid companion, and Miss Sandringham and I are on the best of terms."

"Are you? And what, may I ask, are those terms? How much does she pay you?"

By this time Sophie was quite alert to the game and answered readily: "Oh, but I could not reveal that, your ladyship. That is a matter strictly between Miss Sandringham and me. If the matter is of interest to you, your ladyship, may I suggest that you speak to my mistress about it?"

"But what if I suddenly felt the need of a paid companion and liked very much to hire you for myself? I could hardly take the matter up with your mistress now, could I?"

"Well, in that case, I fear you would be wasting your breath, your ladyship, for I could never leave Miss Sandringham. You see, I love her as though she were my own sister."

The countess regarded Sophie with a shrewd look in her eye. Then she slowly nodded her head and said: "Yes, I think it is so, Miss Sandringham. For I am sure your name never was Grantford."

The color came to Sophie's cheeks, and she knew that she was unmasked. There was nothing she could say and she hung her head.

"So you *are* a Miss Sandringham, every bit as much as your sister with the veil. Since we have come so far, I pray you will tell me the reason why your sister covers her face."

Sophie raised her head and said: "My lady, you have found us out, and I would not prolong this unhappy conversation. I can assure you that my sister joins me in thanking you for your kind hospitality. Please pass my regrets to Mr. Linscombe—oh, dear, he is a lord, isn't he? The earl's brother?"

"The earl."

"The earl?"

"Yes, my dear. Mr. Linscombe is the right honorable earl of Leighton, my only son."

"Why, he is even more unassuming than Alan, and Alan never was an earl until just recently."

"Alan?"

"Yes. He is married to my sister Pennie. She is a countess, too, because she married Alan, and he is the earl of Dalby, you see."

"Indeed I do—and I am beginning to wonder how two young ladies of such excellent connections are gadding about the country, completely unescorted."

"Oh!" gasped Sophie. "You are not fair, my lady. You are getting all our secrets! Please, as we have accepted your hospitality under false pretenses, we must not trouble you further but proceed to take our leave of you."

"Nonsense, child! Not when it has just begun to be so very interesting! Oh, do sit down and let us chat! Stop trying to pretend you are any sort of a servant, you just are not cut out for it."

Sophie slowly sank into a chair and asked, uncertainly: "What do you think John—I mean, Mr. Lin—er—that is, my lord earl will have to say to it?"

"I think he will be charmed with it all. You have nothing to worry about, child. Now, I think it is time to have this other Miss Sandringham down and see if we cannot solve the rest of the mystery. Pray, how is she called?"

"She is my sister Sarah, my lady," replied Sophie, quite resigned.

Her ladyship raised a hand to the bellrope by her chair and tugged at it.

Sarah came into the room looking at Sophie, but as the veil completely hid her expression, she could not send a look of inquiry to her sister. As she came to stand in front of the countess, her posture bespoke wariness.

Sophie rose and said: "Countess Leighton, I present my sister Sarah."

She turned and saw Sarah standing as though stricken, and cried: "Sarah! Where are your manners? You have just been presented to a countess!"

Sarah's manner was that of someone dazed as she slowly curtsied to her ladyship and said in a very little voice: "I am honored, my lady."

Said Sophie: "And you might as well have done with the veil. Her ladyship will not rest until you do."

"Does she know all about us? Did you have to tell her everything?"

"I tried not to, I swear it, but she was too clever for me—and anyway, we never planned that we should have to play-act the parts. Could you have done it any better, do you think?"

Sarah shrugged: "Well, it is your business, not mine. I was only trying to help you. I shall be glad to get rid of this thing in any case," she ended as she slipped off the veil.

Now it was her ladyship's turn to gasp. "Oh, great heavens, what have we here?" Her eyes traveled rapidly back and forth between the twins, her expression one of almost shock.

It took a little time before she was able to recover her composure. "Well, now," she said, "I begin to see the necessity for the veil if you were bound to travel alone. But, for the life of me, I cannot see the necessity."

Sophie said: "In a sense we were running away, my lady. You see, my fiancé is something afraid of his father, and it is necessary that I go to speak with the gentleman with regard to our troth. Actually, there is not a thing wrong with Oliver, it is just that he fears he can not make his father listen to him and must seek support from my brother-in-law, the earl. Well, as it happens, Lord Dalby is a justice of the King's Bench, newly appointed and not able to give his immediate attention to our problem with Mr. Grantford."

"I see. And you, therefore, found it necessary to go to Mr. Grantford, the father, to ask for his son's hand in marriage."

"Precisely. You are so understanding, my lady."

"Oh, my poor John!" exclaimed the countess. Then she took another look at the pair of sisters and looked up to heaven. "Oh, my poor John!" she exclaimed once again.

The twins exchanged puzzled glances.

Just then Lord Leighton came into the room. He was smiling as he entered, but when he saw what awaited him, the smile faded from his face and he came to a stop.

"Great Scott! What have we here!" he exclaimed, his eyes traveling rapidly back and forth between the twins. Then the smile came back to his lips and he laughed. "How very marvelous!"

He turned to Sarah and bowed. "My dear Miss Sandringham, has any one ever told you how remarkably close is the resemblance between you and your sister Sophie?"

Sophie leaped from her seat and cried: "He knew!" She turned to Sarah. "He knew at a glance!"

Lord Leighton laughed. "Really, my dear, it was not so awfully difficult. You are wearing the attendant's gown and your sister, the lady's. It was nothing more than that."

Sophie's face fell in disappointment as she resumed her seat.

His lordship turned to his mother. "You have gone to work with your usual inimitable style, I see. I pray no one suffered any embarrassment."

"I am too skillful for that, my son—but I could not sit still until I had got to the bottom of it. Now, as my reward, allow me to present these ladies to you. My lord earl, these are the ladies Sandringham, Miss Sophie and Miss Sarah. They are sisters to Lady Dalby?"—she looked to Sophie, who nodded—"countess of Dalby by marriage to Alan, the earl, and a new member of the King's Bench Court—a most awesome connection, I must say. And pray, what of your parents, my dears? Who may they be?"

It seemed that Sophie was elected spokeswoman and she went on: "Papa is a judge in the shires where we reside. Woodhouse in Leicestershire to be exact, and Mama is a Dampier."

His lordship bowed to the ladies. "My very great pleasure. I am so happy that I found you."

"And," added the countess, dryly, "they have

gone off on their own so that Miss Sophie may have an opportunity to ask for her fiancé's hand in marriage from his father—"

"What!" exploded the earl. "You cannot be serious!"

Sophie, looking stormy, retorted: "I most certainly am!"

"Oh, you *cannot* be serious! What sort of a man is it who lets his fiancée speak for him! Is he a man at all?"

"Oh, you do not understand how it is! Oliver is as much a man as any of them! It is just that he has this inability to speak with his father at the moment! Oh, he will! I assure you he will—or would have eventually—but I am not about to sit upon my thumbs and wait. My sister is all set, and we would be married at the same time. If I were to wait for Oliver, I am sure Sarah would be celebrating her first-born before ever Oliver and I exchanged our vows at the altar. What is so exceptional in that?"

The look on his lordship's face was a strange one. It grew even stranger when her ladyship remarked with a chuckle: "I imagine that the chaise will be ready sooner than any of us might have expected, my lord."

He threw a stormy look at his mother and stalked out of the room.

Chapter 8

The twins spent the little that was left of the morning with the dowager, during which time they learned that his lordship, in the early years of his marriage, had lost his wife in unsuccessful childbirth. From that time he had devoted himself to raising hunters and racing mounts as a way to take his mind off his sorrow. It had worked out quite well in that Linscombe mounts commanded excellent prices and brought a most excellent income to the estate. She was quick to point out that the Linscombe rents were more than enough by themselves to insure their wealth, for they owned most of the land on which Linsdale and Leighton Buzzard stood, not to say anything of their vast holdings scattered over the countryside. But it was nice that his lordship had found something to occupy him, so much better than if he had betaken himself to London's gaming tables or worse—as so many wealthy young men of his ilk had been doing since time immemorial to assuage grief or disappointment.

In turn, the twins spoke of their life in Woodhouse, their love of horses and, of course, the great stir they had caused in London with their recent coming out.

"I dare say you will be rushing back to the city to continue with your triumphs there," suggested the countess.

Sarah shook her head. "I do not think so. After all, we are satisfied that we have found our future husbands and, since we always cause a stir wherever we go, it has become something of a bore, don't you know. As a matter of fact, Sophie and I have agreed not to trade upon our resemblance to each other any longer. For the longest time, it was all sorts of fun, but now we are grown ladies, and that sort of business one grows out of."

"Then you will not be going back to London?"

Sophie sighed. "Oh, I suppose we shall have to. When Pennie and Alan catch up with us, they will insist upon it—"

"Well, of course, my lady," Sarah interrupted her sister, "I have every intention of returning to London. My fiancé is to be clerk to Alan in King's Bench Court, and so we shall be settling in the city. I have come along with Sophie only so that she could travel to see her future father-in-law."

"Obviously, you love each other dearly. I marvel

that you can contemplate this separation that your marriages will force upon you—or shall your husband—Oliver, is it?—also find his future in the city?" her ladyship asked of Sophie.

Sophie frowned. "My lady, that is a problem to which I have not the answer. I am not sure what Oliver intends, for I do not believe that he is particularly sure of it himself. It is a worry. I should hate to have to be apart from Sarah, but we cannot have everything our way now, can we?"

"Indeed, you are very wise, child. Well, I must say I cannot remember when I have ever enjoyed the company of two such charming and interesting guests. I pray that, if ever you are in the neighborhood again, you will not hesitate to drop in on this old lady."

"Oh, thank you, my lady. Indeed, we would not miss it!" said Sophie with enthusiasm.

"Now, I think it is time for a bit of lunch. Dear me, how very thoughtless of me! Have you had anything to eat at all this morning?"

"Oh, yes, we had a roll and a spot of tea at some inn just outside London—not to say that we could not do justice to something hearty at the moment."

At that moment, his lordship came back in, and there was a strained look in his eyes.

"Your ladyship, ladies, I offer my apologies for my boorish behavior when I departed your company so abruptly. I pray you will forgive me and allow me the enjoyment of your company at lunch."

"As I am your mother, forgiveness comes easily to me, my lord. How say you, ladies? Can you for-

give the earl his bad manners before company?"
asked the countess in a bantering tone.

"Of course, my lord," responded Sarah. "I am
sure we hardly noticed."

His lordship winced a bit at that, and he looked
to Sophie for her response.

She was not up to saying anything. She only
nodded, even as her cheeks took on a pinkish hue.

His lordship appeared more than satisfied, and
immediately the situation was eased as he escorted
the ladies to the dining room.

By the dint of throwing out leads in the conversation, the countess, one way or another, managed
to get the girls to repeat all they had told her, toss-
ing wise looks at her son every now and then. As he
exchanged looks with his mother, gratitude was in
his eyes. He obviously found the conversation of
the greatest interest.

Although Sarah was not all that interested and
tended to listen rather than talk, Sophie, on the
other hand, went to great lengths to satisfy his lordship's curiosity and did so, charmingly and wittily,
he responding in kind.

As lunch came to an end and the earl had to
leave them for the paddocks, there was a mutual regret felt between him and Sophie that they should
part. And it was sensed by the countess and Sarah
as well.

As her son left them, her ladyship sat back in her
chair, a very thoughtful expression on her face.

Sarah was frowning and studying Sophie, obviously not able to make up her mind. She reached to her side to take Sophie's hand in hers and received a squeeze for her effort. They had got to talk.

The opportunity came quickly when the countess announced the lunch at an end and rose. "It is time for me to take a bit of rest. I am sure you girls have a bit to do. You will be staying the night, I have no doubt. So do you make yourselves comfortable and come to me for a chat when the sun is low. If you like, why do you not go about the grounds? We have some very pretty gardens. It is not all horses with us, you know— Oh, and yes, as you are both horsewomen, you might like to go for a canter in the morning. We have a selection of the most excellent ladies' mounts. If I can handle them, any female can."

"Are you not given to riding, my lady?" asked Sophie. "With all the riding stock about, I should think you would be."

"No, I am never so expert. Nor was Lady Martha and, perhaps, that lack in her may have contributed to the tragedy. She had a fall early in her marriage to John. The doctors had a suspicion that it may have made for complications when it came time for her to bear—oh, we shall never know for sure, but my son can never forget it. I dare say that his next wife, if there is ever to be one, will have to be very much at home up on a horse. You see, Martha was not."

With that she left the twins to their own devices and retired to her chambers.

Their room had been completely refreshed and made ready for their stay. Their few belongings had been put away neatly, and the pair of dresses they had each brought, newly pressed. The twins could not help but be pleased with the consideration shown them.

They inspected everything, holding hands as they went about the room. It was very well furnished and in a style they felt Pennie would not have found exceptional.

"I think I should like to have a room like this in my house some day," said Sophie.

"Then why do you not settle for this room. All you have got to do is to marry Lord Leighton, my dear," responded Sarah with a little laugh.

"Sarah, I do not find that remark in the least humorous."

"Well, now, I wonder why you do not. I have been meaning to speak to you for some time now. I am beginning to suspect that you gave us away because you wanted to."

"Why ever in the world should I?"

"Because you find his lordship marvelously attractive."

"I most certainly do not!"

"How odd. I certainly do. Come now, Sophie, you are not being honest with me and it hurts me. This is no time for us to hide from each other. We have never done so before."

"Very well, his lordship is, indeed, quite attractive. There, does that satisfy you?"

"But what of Oliver?"

"I have admitted that Lord Leighton is an attractive gentleman. That is not to say that Oliver is not—nor does it imply anything else."

"Well, Sophie, if you say it is so. But I could swear that, given a chance, his lordship would dangle after you in a minute."

"That has nothing to say how I feel about his lordship. But, I say, Sarah, have you noticed that his lordship has not the least difficulty in distinguishing between us?"

"Really, Sophie, what has he to be confused about? We are in different dress. It would not be the same if we were dressing alike now, would it?"

A smile played about Sophie's mouth as she thought about it. "I would certainly like to see if it did. I truly would."

"Well, it is quite out of the question, my dear. We have not got two things alike between us. Remember we did it on purpose not to be recognized for twins."

"Still, that should not present us with any difficulty. All we need do is to exchange our costumes—and we can do it right now. Then we can go out to the paddock to inspect the mounts, you know—for tomorrow's ride."

"Oh, are we going for a ride tomorrow? We have not even discussed it."

"Well, her ladyship as much as told us to. It would hardly show appreciation of their hospitality if we were to decline after she suggested it."

"Sophie, you are up to something. I thought we

were now grown too old to indulge in the nonsense of our childhood."

"Oh, this once will not hurt anything. Are you not curious in the least? I mean to say it is so rare that anyone can distinguish us on such short notice. I think Alan was the only one thus far. Why even our fiancés had all sorts of trouble with us and for years, if I suspect rightly."

"Well, Percy came to it quite naturally. He did it all by himself, once he set his mind to it."

"I am not disparaging Percy, Sarah. I just have a wish to see if the earl, our host, resembles Alan in his ability to know us right off. Come, let us make the exchange and go right down. I mean to say it will not be an embarrassment if he fails. You can go right on being me, and I can go right on being you until we are alone and can change back. He need never know that we have switched ourselves."

"But what of Oliver?"

"What of Oliver?"

"You are not answering me, love. Here we are, disporting ourselves on this great estate, and you have got this purpose to accomplish with Mr. Grantford. Pray, what do you think that our lady sister is doing right now? Do you think that she is sitting idly by, waiting for us to return to Cavendish Square? You know she is not. I will lay odds that she is sending out to scour the roads about London. You know Pennie! She is probably hot after us herself and, by this time, has reckoned where we are off to and why. Sophie, we are wasting time!"

"I do not care! For one thing, Pennie will never

find us here. I am sure that she has never heard of Linscombe Park, and furthermore, we have not got our transportation. If you do not recall, I shall gladly remind you that the chaise is broken down and in need of a new rear wheel. It rests now, I am sure, in some shop in Linslade with who knows how many mechanics and 'prentices rushing madly to and fro to restore it. I am sure they are rushing because the earl has taken an interest in it, and he does not appear to me to be a gentleman whom anyone would dare to cross."

"After that testimonial to our gracious host, I begin to tremble for Oliver's hopes for you. My, how very impressed you are with his lordship."

"If you will but admit it, so are you!"

"Of course I am. But I would not trade Percy for him!"

"I would!"

"What! You would trade Oliver for the earl and you are engaged to him?"

"No, silly, but I would trade Percy for him," retorted Sophie with a laugh.

Sarah laughed with her.

"I feel better now," said Sarah after a bit. "I had a fear that you were forgetting your pledge to Oliver. Now we must urge his lordship to see us on our way as quickly as possible."

"I am sure that he is doing all in his power in that regard. He did say it would take a little time, and as long as we have the time, I do not see any sense in our staying cooped up in the house. Come, Sarah, let us exchange our clothes and go out to him. It will be, at the least, an innocent amusement to help us pass the time."

Sarah reluctantly agreed, and in a little while they were prepared to go out on the grounds for a look about.

The grounds of Linscombe Park were very nicely laid out. Everything was in perfect order and on the classical style. There were a number of stone creations scattered over the lawn, each surrounded by its own little garden filled with colorful flowers. There were statuary and pergolas and pavillions with little walks of Portland stone connecting one with another; in short, a most romantic setting. Although Beaumanor had a finer house, its grounds, carelessly tended for years, were disordered by comparison, and the Leicestershire setting was so much wilder with great Charnwood Forest brooding down upon the earl of Dalby's hunting estate. Linscombe Park was a most peaceful scene.

The twins strolled across the lawn and down behind the house. They could see the paddock area and the stables laid out before them. There were far more buildings assembled than were ever needed for the care and maintenance of even a very respectable string of hunters, and they were quite impressed with it. Obviously the earl of Leighton had a great investment in horseflesh to require so many structures, and as the countess had indicated, it must pay him a handsome return or he could not afford all the land that was set aside for his stock.

They came to stand by the paddock rail and

watch. Within, his lordship and his head groom were inspecting a fine looking mount. It was fully saddled and stood patiently as the two men went over it thoroughly and with great care. No one noticed that they had visitors.

"May we come inside?" called out Sophie.

At once the two men turned from the horse, and the earl, a smile on his face, came walking over to them. As he opened the gate he looked sharply at them and chuckled. "Indeed, I never thought about it, but it must be quite confusing to be twins. Here, you have gone and got your costumes mixed up! If I did not have such a sharp eye for horses and the ladies, perhaps not quite in that order, it is I who would have been confused."

Sophie bit her lip and blushed. Sarah smiled and looked down.

"Ah, Miss Sophie, do I detect a plot? I suspect that you did it on purpose to test me, did you not?"

Sophie giggled and nodded. "I pray you will forgive us, my lord."

"Naught to forgive. I am charmed that you should have tried. We were just looking over one of the mounts. It has been sold to a gentleman in Surrey. We wish to be sure that it is in perfect condition."

"It appears so to me. Oh, it is a beauty!" exclaimed Sophie, going over to the great fellow and rubbing his silken nose. "My, how gentle he is!"

"Thank you, Miss Sophie. Would you care to ride him?"

"Thank you, my lord, but I am not dressed for it.

I should be delighted to try him tomorrow morning if you would allow it."

His lordship's face fell. "I fear you will not be with us for long enough tomorrow. I have been given to understand that the chaise will be ready to proceed by then."

Now it was Sophie's face that filled with disappointment.

His lordship hurried on to say: "Of course, that is only what I have heard. It could be delayed as much as twenty-four hours for all anyone truly knows. Buckingham mechanics are not always up to their estimates—I am sure you have run into that sort of thing in Leicestershire, have you not?"

"Oh, all the time, my lord!" said Sophie quickly. Sarah raised her eyes to the skies and turned away to hide a smile.

"Well, then, I think we can take it for granted that the chaise will be somewhat delayed, can't we? Miss Sophie, Miss Sarah, I should be delighted to have your company for a canter tomorrow morning. Come and look over the mounts. You may take your choice of the lot. You will find they are all of them choice specimens and you cannot make a poor selection."

Chapter 9

Lady Dalby learned it was not an easy thing for a countess to embark on a swift journey at a moment's notice. Although the decision that she should go after the runaways was reached rather quickly, it was quite another thing to set out upon the search. First, to insure that all respect was paid to her along the road, it was necessary to have the Desford traveling coach brought out and refurbished, making sure that the coat-of-arms, wherever it appeared on the vehicle, could be easily discerned. That called for a bit more than cleaning and polishing. A spot of paint, here and there, was definitely required, the coach having been kept in the rear stables, out of the way, as too cumbersome for use in the city. Naturally, such neglect had in no way preserved its appearance.

Then there was a question of retinue. Lord Dalby was all for two footmen and two lady's-maids to go along, but Lady Dalby held out for one of each retainer on the grounds that so many people would not make for a very quick run. Fortunately, neither Oliver nor Percy boasted a valet, so that left the party something less than a crowd. As the great carriage could hold six in comfort, her ladyship, her maid and the two young gentlemen were able to travel without feeling cramped for space. The footman joined the coachman on the box.

Then, of course, there was the question of what luggage to take along. Lady Dalby did not reckon on more than a day or two on the road, time enough to get to Woodhouse, where she had a number of things still in her parents' cottage, Bellflower, and then there was something more at Beaumanor, the Desford estate, practically next door—if one did not count the great length of driveway before one reached the mansion.

Lord Dalby, however, was not sanguine about the time that the trip would require, so that the cavernous boot of the carriage was quite well filled with parcels, and my lady's pocketbook with banknotes.

Lord Dalby also cautioned his lady to never hesitate to send him an express in the event she had the slightest need of him to hurry back, for he was already missing her and she not even started.

There was an exchange of affectionate salutes at parting, and at last, the expedition was on its way.

Lady Dalby's idea was to check at the various tollgates along the road to Leicestershire and, in that way, gain some idea of both the correctness of their route and of the time they were behind the fugitives. They were in the greatest luck, for at the very first tollgate, they received information regarding the twins. It was Oliver who made inquiry, but it was Lady Dalby who extracted the information from his confusion.

"Well, Oliver, what have you found out?" asked Lady Dalby, all anxiety.

"Nothing of any use, my lady," replied Oliver with a very disappointed look. "I regret to say there has been no sign of them."

"Oh, but I cannot believe it! They had nowhere else to go. They have got to have passed this way. What did the keeper say?"

"No one fitting their description passed through this gate this day or any day that he can recall. I mean to say a pair of twins are bound to be remembered and two such beauties as Sophie and Sarah—well, I say!"

"Oh, you numbskull! Has it ever occurred to you that the girls would have taken some pains to disguise the fact that they are twins? Did he say if anyone has passed through early? Two women traveling alone?"

"Well, he did say something to that effect. It was about six that a lady and her maid came through in a post chaise— Oh, I say!"

"Yes, of course—"

But Oliver was now too excited to stop. "—And one of them—the lady—had on a heavy veil!"

"There! What did I tell you! Percy, signal the coachman to hurry on!"

But when they stopped to calculate how far they were behind Sarah and Sophie, the sense of exultation rapidly diminished. If the twins had passed through that first tollgate at six o'clock in the morning and they had come through it at some minutes before twelve, then they were six hours behind. At the next stop, Lady Dalby consulted with the coachman. He gave her encouragement. There was every chance that they would come up with the girls this side of Leicester. They were driving three pair and they were stalwart beasts as against the two pair of broken-down post nags drawing the chaise. They could stop and give their animals a breather, but they would never have to change teams, for he could drive them at a pretty pace without ever blowing them up. Her ladyship was not to worry.

They proceeded on, and indeed the coachman's boast seemed to be coming true. They came through Linslade only four hours behind the girls. But when they arrived in Bletchley, dismal disappointment awaited them. The trail was lost. The girls had not come through the gate.

Lady Dalby could not understand it. Surely, Sarah and Sophie were making their way to Bell-flower or Beaumanor, and they must have gotten this far. Even if they were four hours behind the girls, still the trail should not have ended. There was no reason in the world that they would have taken another route.

Neither Percy nor Oliver proved the slightest help in this impasse. Their expressions bespoke their extreme unhappiness and their unrelieved concern. They had nothing to suggest, and after a few dismal comments from Oliver, her ladyship begged him to shut up and allow her to think. Finally, after reviewing their progress in the greatest detail to assure herself that they could not have possibly overrun the twins, her ladyship came to a decision.

"We are going on! There is no question in my mind that Sarah and Sophie are headed for Woodhouse. It makes no sense that they should attempt any other place. I admit that I have yet to fathom their purpose in this trip of theirs, but they must to Woodhouse, of that I am positive. Therefore, it behooves us to go there, too."

"But, my lady, what if they are not there? Where do we look next?" asked Percy. "Oh, pray that they have not taken it into their heads to hide themselves because they have had second thoughts as to the desirability of our marrying them!" he almost wailed.

"Percy, I pray you will not fret yourself. It is early days to speculate upon anything so incredible. Neither Sophie nor Sarah are afraid to speak their minds. If they had any reservations about wedding you, they would have said so. No, it has got to be something else. We shall only learn it when we find them."

"But what if they are not there?"

"Then I must place the matter into the hands of my lord. He can muster the forces of the kingdom in our behalf, I am sure. You, Percy, you are acquainted with these matters, since you have an interest in them. What recourse has my lord?"

"Why, he can confer with the magistrate at Bow Street. The runners are past expert in such cases. Perhaps we should have called the runners into it sooner."

"I sincerely hope not. Oh, I shall never forgive myself if it truly was a nefarious business from the start— Oh, but it cannot be! You are making an old woman of me! Let us stop this sniveling and be on our way!"

The signal was given, and they passed on through Bletchley, going north.

The next morning saw the twins up and about well before six o'clock. The countess had allowed them each to borrow a pair of riding habits of hers from her younger days, and the fit was not all that bad. In any case, they would be riding on the estate and would not be meeting with anyone, so it made little difference. Riding boots were a problem, for they had not brought any along with them, and those belonging to her ladyship were just too small. His lordship had come to the rescue last evening by showing them how to wrap canvas about their lower limbs to serve as protection to the calf. As their riding skirts hid most of it and they were not going to make their appearance in Hyde Park on Rotten Row, it, too, made little difference.

As they dressed themselves in the borrowed and makeshift getups, Sophie suggested: "You do not have to go, Sarah. I mean to say, if you are fatigued from our journey, I would not resent it if you wished to stay behind and rest."

Sarah replied: "Heavens, Sophie, I am not in the least fatigued and I am looking forward to a ride. Do you realize that we have not been on a horse since we left Woodhouse? I am going to take a mount into Charley Forest while you go to call upon Mr. Grantford."

"Oh, Sarah, I do wish you would not harp on the subject. Sufficient unto the day the evil thereof . . . or some such thing."

Sarah ceased in her wrapping of the canvas about her leg and looked up at Sophie. "What an awful thing to say! Evil, Sophie? The day you speak to Mr. Grantford? How can you feel it is in any way evil? I do not understand you!"

"Oh, I was just trying to be emphatic. I will admit my choice of quotation was something poor. But what I mean to say is that I do not see the need of speaking about it while we are here. We shall come to it soon enough. Why cannot we forget the business for a bit and enjoy ourselves?"

"I begin to worry about you. I am not enjoying myself, no matter what you think. I would much rather be back in Cavendish Square with Percy. I dare say the poor dear is worrying himself sick over my disappearance. Now, Sophie, we are going for a ride with his lordship just to pass the time that we must endure until the chaise is ready to proceed. That is all—or do you have some other idea? Is that why you suggested that I stay behind? Sophie, I am shocked! What of Oliver?"

"Sarah, if you persist in nagging at me, I swear you shall go alone with his lordship. You are seeing a great deal more in this than there is. I was merely being sisterly and concerned for your welfare."

"And I thank you, sister dear, but, as there is not a farthing's worth of difference between us, you know very well that I am no more fatigued than are you. I have exerted myself in no way that you have not. Now, I suggest that we go to meet his lordship and take the opportunity to urge him to see us off in the *bloody* chaise!"

"Sarah! Your language!"

"Well, that is how I feel!"

They had been riding for more than an hour and still had not been over more than a fraction of the park. Unlike the grounds that surrounded Beaumanor, which were wild and unruly, all of Linscombe Park seemed to be fairly level and accessible to a horse and rider. There were well-trodden bridle paths if one wanted to just let the horse wander, but for a more exciting ride, one could venture out cross-country and feel reasonably sure that there were no great surprises in store for an unwary rider.

Neither Sophie nor Sarah had aught to complain about as to the terrain, and even less as to the conduct of their host. The sun was now well up, and the air was beginning to get warm, but they never noticed, giving all of their attention to Lord Leighton, who appeared bent upon charming them. There was nothing flamboyant in his manner, for it was quiet, and perhaps, it was his mild way that made his witty remarks sound so very acute and humorous, too. There was an easy feeling of companionship amongst them as they slowed their mounts down to a walk and Lord Leighton said: "We have been in the saddle a bit longer than I had planned. I pray I have not overtired you. Just a little way from here is some shade beside a small stream. It is an excellent place to rest our mounts and ourselves—or we can start back for the stables now. We are not so faraway."

Sarah was about to suggest they go back, for his lordship had said that the chaise might be ready to travel a little later on; but Sophie was quicker and expressed a strong wish to rest by the stream. His lordship never consulted Sarah's wishes in the matter but began at once to lead the way. Sarah sighed resignedly and followed her sister, who was riding at his lordship's side and a little back.

It was a lovely spot he led them to, just the right place to rest, with plenty of shade provided by a scattering of oaks, and water for the horses. Sophie exclaimed: "Oh, how delightful! A perfect place for a picnic!"

"My dear, if I can prevail upon you to stay with us another day, it could be easily arranged," he said.

But this was too much for Sarah who replied before Sophie had a chance to: "It is most kind of you, my lord, and I could wish that we had the time to spare, but we are overdue in Woodhouse as it is. In fact, at this very minute we should have been coming through the gates of Beaumanor. Indeed, my lord, it has been most pleasant, our stay with the countess and you, but we may not tarry longer."

Lord Leighton nodded and said: "Of course, I understand your haste, Miss Sarah, and I do not wish to hold you. What I can do is to send you off in one of my carriages for you to take care of your business while Miss Sophie remains with us."

"My lord, I fear you misunderstand. It is not *my* business but Sophie's upon which we are embarked. Sophie, will you not say a word?"

The reluctance with which Sophie agreed with Sarah was apparent to his lordship and to Sarah.

Lord Leighton dismounted and, masking his disappointment, remarked: "Ah, yes, I had forgotten. You have got an interview with your prospective father-in-law."

Sophie's face fell as he went first to Sarah and made a step for her with his hands so that she could dismount. Next he came to her and, as she disengaged herself from the sidesaddle rests, instead of making a step for her, he held up his arms. It was such an inviting prospect that Sophie, without hesitation, entrusted herself to him and was brought to her feet in a strong yet gentle embrace. For a moment, they were face to face, and Sophie experienced a sudden weakness in the knees that oddly enough left her breathless into the bargain. He began to ease his hold of her, but as she appeared to be a little unsteady, he quickly restored his arms to their former position and helped her to a spot under a nearby tree.

Sophie, her face very pink from all that exertion, sat down and, looking up at him with a bright smile, said: "I fear I was more fatigued than I knew, my lord. Thank you so very *much!*"

Sarah surrendered her horse to his lordship and took a seat beside her sister. She was feeling quite frustrated, having missed nothing of the exchange between Sophie and Lord Leighton. She was of a mind to accept his lordship's offer of transportation except she would return to London and leave Sophie behind at Linscombe Park. But a picture of Oliver's disappointed face and the impossible explanations she would be called upon to make quite dissuaded her from that course. Somehow she had got to bring Sophie to an awareness of the fact that this was no time for an idle flirtation. One had to order one's affairs and take care of the important things before any others. The thought made her uncomfortable, for Percy was the most important thing in her own life and she had no business being in Buckinghamshire while he remained in London.

Still, there was nothing that she could do about it at the moment, so rather than ruin a perfectly lovely morning by scrapping with Sophie, she signaled her disapproval to her sister by her silence.

Sophie was too deep in conversation with his lordship to remark her sister's discontent and felt very much at ease, nay, happy, that there was this pleasant time to enjoy before they must be on their way again.

After making a few abortive attempts to have Sarah join in the conversation, Lord Leighton devoted his attention to the one he considered the far more charming of the sisters, and the time sped swiftly by. Finally, Sarah, quite bored with it all, suggested that they go down to the stream and try wading about in it, it looked so refreshingly clear.

Lord Leighton immediately arose to assist the ladies, but Sophie grabbed him by the hand and pulled him back down beside her, saying: "I am not in a mood, Sarah dear, but I pray you will not be deterred if that is what you prefer."

"Well, just for a bit—but, Sophie, need I remind you that time is wasting and we should be on our way?"

With that she turned about and went to sit beside the stream, staring into its limpid waters, trying to understand what had come over her sister.

The conversation taking place under the oak tree went on for a while. Sophie spoke of her days spent with her sister, of many of the pranks that they had played, even how they had managed to get an earl for their sister—although, she was careful to explain, she was never that sure that their help in Pennie's cause had been all that essential.

Lord Leighton encouraged her to talk and managed to get her on to the subject of her fiancé by inquiring as to Sarah's young gentleman. The conversation flowed to the subject of Oliver quite smoothly.

"I know you do not think well of Oliver, but then you have never met him," said Sophie, in an almost argumentative tone. "It is just that he has not come into his own as yet, and his father is something overbearing. If only Oliver could come to a decision as to how he plans to spend his years, I am sure everything would work itself out on the instant. Oliver was not the brightest pupil at school and he has but recently finished his studies, so it is no wonder that he is at loose ends and not in a way to impress his father, don't you see. I know it sounds as though he is a bit weak, and, mayhap, even foolish at times, but the thing is I love him anyway and that is what counts in the end."

"I see," said Lord Leighton. "The chap is not much in most departments but is a romantic sort to have captured your heart."

"Oliver, romantic? Oh, I say, you do not know Oliver! No, I am sure he is not romantic, he is too concerned with his troubles to be romantic. For one thing he is not at all sure of himself—but then he is still quite young and my sister and I browbeat both boys unmercifully during all the years of our childhood."

His lordship smiled and remarked, offhandedly: "I imagine you still can manage to browbeat the poor fellow."

Sophie laughed: "Well, of course!"

"I marvel that you can love a one such as he," said the earl in a low voice, shifting his seat upon the ground so that he wound up much closer to her.

Sophie, feeling a little breathless at his proximity, turned to look at him and found herself staring into a pair of dark eyes that seemed to reach deep into her soul.

She took a quick breath and started to move back from him only to find his arms suddenly about her, pulling her close to him. She was about to cry out but instantly thought better of it and relaxed in his arms as his lips bore down upon hers.

She was sure that she was going to enjoy the experience and was planning the set-down she would deliver to him after it was over. But it never got beyond the planning stage. Her thoughts became incoherent as his lips demanded that she respond to him, blotting out all her thinking so that only feelings deep and rich remained to her—but they were all she could have asked. She wanted no more than this. She wanted much more than this. Her lips signaled her passion, and her arms clung to him with a desperation of desire she had never known.

The sudden stillness after the light hum of conversation under the oak tree intruded on Sarah's thoughts and she turned around. It gave her quite a start to see Sophie in the passionate embrace of his lordship.

Her first intention was to interrupt this unseemly behavior. She even began to rise from her seat beside the stream. Then she shook her head and resumed her former posture of contemplation. What was the use? Sophie knew her own mind, and if she had a wish to find herself in the arms of the earl of Leighton, well, Oliver had better look out for himself. Of course, it was bound to add up to another delay, and that she could not thank Sophie for.

Suddenly she found herself wondering just how *had* Oliver spent his time with his fiancée. Not to any great purpose, it seemed. Now, Percy . . .

She was smiling dreamily when she heard Sophie call to her and say did not she think it was time they returned.

Chapter 10

Never trust a coachman's estimate of his horse's stamina. It will always be an overestimate, thought Lady Dalby as she sat in an inn just outside Wootton. The horses were definitely winded, even before they had got this far, and they had had to limp into this tiny inn. Wouldn't you know there were no fresh horses to be had nor had there ever been? All the staging took place in Northampton, just a few miles farther north. Just a few miles farther and they could have hired a fresh team and been on their way with a minimum loss of time. Now they had no recourse but to stop for hours, for all she knew, to rest up the beasts. In fact, it was so late in the day that there was no point in proceeding until tomorrow. Oh, how ashamed Alan would be of her if he knew that on their first day out they had not gotten so far as Northampton!

She pulled herself together and ordered Percy to hire them a rig to carry them to the Angel in Northampton. They would stay the night, by which time the horses would be sufficiently rested to complete the journey. The present establishments were hardly up to their requirements for a night's lodging.

Percy appeared to hesitate. "Er—my lady, may I make a suggestion?"

"Yes, Percy. What is it?"

"It pains me to propose that Oliver go on ahead. But I have given the matter my most serious consideration. If he were to go on ahead in the rig we hire, then someone will be there to see to the twins. I would much rather it were I, of course, but one of us must remain with you, my lady—and I regret to say that it must be I, for Oliver has the greater problem, what with his parent. It might give him an opportunity to come to terms with Mr. Grantford. In any case, I could wish that one of us would go on ahead as quickly as possible."

Her ladyship studied the pained expression on Percy's face for a moment. "Yes, Percy, I begin to understand what my lord has seen in you. You do have a surprising capacity for clear thinking."

"Thank you, my lady," he said with a little bow, his face easing a little.

Oliver did not trust himself to speak. It was all up to Lady Dalby. One of them had to remain with her—and she had purse and purse strings, whereas both Percy and he were light of pocket in the extreme.

"Oliver, you have heard. Will you be the one to go?" asked her ladyship.

"Oh, yes, my lady!"

"Then that is how we shall do it."

While the twins were having their outing with Lord Leighton, and Lady Dalby and Percy were just starting out on the last leg of their journey from the Angel in Northampton, a weary Oliver drove his hired rig onto the grounds of the Grantford residence in Woodhouse. He had driven most of the night.

A young lad came running up to take hold of his horse, and he stepped down from the gig, almost staggering from the weight of fatigue. He caught himself, doffed his hat to brush back his hair, a few locks of which had fallen forward over his brow, straightened up his coat and turned to the boy.

"The rig was hired in Wootton. See what can be done about having it returned. Is the master at home?"

"Yes, Mr. Oliver. He be in a sour humor this day."

"When is he not! Bah!" he exclaimed and went into the house.

He broke in upon his father having breakfast.

Mr. Grantford looked up at the interruption, grunted and turned his gaze back to the morning journal he was perusing.

"Wind in the wrong quarter as usual, sir?" asked Oliver, clenching his hands.

Without looking up, Mr. Grantford asked: "Had your breakfast, puppy?"

"No, sir, I have not had my breakfast. I had to travel quickly."

"I do not see why—but as you are here and breakfast is served, sit."

"As I have said, I have not the time, sir. Have you by any chance heard if the Sandringham sisters are returned to the neighborhood?"

"The twins?"

"Aye, the twins, if you prefer."

"Burn you, boy! Say the twins if you mean the twins! Must you be forever mealy-mouthed?"

"They are the Sandringham sisters, sir."

"Well, they are not Miss Pennie, and bless me if I care to have them mentioned in the same breath with her. By God, they should have been born boys! They have too much spirit for soft females, more spirit than my own son, blast you!"

"You have not answered my question, sir."

"And what was it? I do not recall that it was of much consequence."

"I desired to know if you had heard that the twins, if you insist, had returned to the vicinity."

"No, I have not and am totally uninterested into the bargain. It has been blessedly peaceful since they departed for London. By the way, cub, where have *you* been all this while? I was sure you had not the funds to be absent from home for so long."

"I shall tell you all about it later. I must go over

to Bellflower Cottage and, if unsuccessful there, to Beaumanor—"

"After your breakfast. Sit, I would talk—"

"It will have to wait. I must leave you now."

"Oliver, I said sit down! Now sit down and do not make me repeat myself."

"Yes, sir—but I wish you would hurry," said Oliver as he fell into a chair alongside the breakfast table.

"Now, eat something. You look peaked. The trouble with you lads is you never stop for a bite when you should. Eat, I say!"

Oliver dutifully picked up a piece of toast and smeared a bit of jelly on it. He took a bite and that appeared to satisfy Mr. Grantford.

"See? You are looking better already. Now, where in blazes have you been?"

"I have been to London."

"Impossible! I know exactly how much I give you and I never gave you as much as a fare to London costs."

"Percy allowed me to go on tick. He covered all my expenses—"

"Damn you for an ungrateful son! Now I am in debt to the viscount! You know how I detest being in debt to anyone."

"No, sir, not to the viscount but to his son Percy. It is Percy's own money that he put out for me."

"That is even more detestable! To be in debt to a young sprout!"

"You need not be, you know. You could be something more generous with me, sir, and you would not have to be in debt to anyone on my account."

"I give you plenty for your needs. More and you would be playing it away at the tables. Is that why you went off to London? By heaven, I shall disown you if you have lost but a farthing at one of those hells!"

"Then my patrimony is secured to me, for I have not squandered a groat in gambling. I have done something far better and far more proper than that."

"Oh, you have, have you?" sneered Mr. Grantford, finally putting down his paper and giving all his attention to Oliver.

"Yes, sir. I have engaged myself to marry Sophie Sandringham."

Mr. Grantford's eyes opened wide, and his face turned to a hue of purple. "I pray, for your sake, that my ears have just deceived me, sir!" he thundered.

"I am sure they did not, sir. I have come for your blessing."

"You have your infernal nerve! How dare you to plight your troth and never a word to me? Am I not to have any say in the choice of *my* daughter-in-law? And what a daughter-in-law! A boy-girl, that is what she is! She and her sister have raised more deviltry in this once-peaceful neighborhood than a band of ruffians. *You* would marry her? I say, can you even tell her apart from her sister—who is not a fig better than she?"

Oliver winced at that. "Look you, sir, I shall marry her whether you approve or not. I love her!"

"And three cheers for his majesty! Bah! You never shall, and I have no wish to waste my breath on the matter."

"But I have pledged my word! Does that not mean anything?"

"Your word? Not a thing! I can see it all as though I had been there. Of course she was sweet to you! You are coming into a fortune, son. There are damn few females who would not be sweet to you if you but gave them a chance. Now, we Grantfords could stand an infusion of bluer blood than we can lay claim to, and I intend that such will be the case. You are not a bad-looking chap, so if you can win yourself a bit of money into the bargain with a bit of excellent bloodline, I would never say no to it—but the Sandringham brats? Never! They are no better blood than ourselves—if as good."

"Well, you must admit that they certainly have got it now—to be allied to the Desfords is nothing to sneeze at."

"They have got it, you simpleton, not you."

"Well, I shall certainly have the connections, shan't I?"

"What connections are you bragging about? Your wife's connections? But they are not even hers. The connections stem from your wife's relations, not yours. They are second-hand connections for you, son, whereas your wife will have the direct connection to the Desfords. Nothing to brag about in my book."

"Oh, damn the connections to hell! That is not what I am marrying Sophie for, anyway!"

"Then it is damn little you are marrying her for, I must say, for you shall have not a penny from me for as long as I live."

"Then I shall sell my prospects to the cents-per-cents!"

"Do that and you shall never see a penny, for I shall disinherit you completely. There is no entail upon my estate. I can bequeath it as I may. When word of that gets around, no cent-per-cent will even bother to give you the time of day, sir!"

"Sir, I never thought I should live to see the day when I would hate my own father."

"Bah! Do not go sentimental on me, boy! You know you won't gain anything by it. I cannot afford the luxury of other fathers, giving in to their offspring all the time. I want to see a Grantford family in being by the time I close my eyes for the last time and I want to see it bolstered with good stock and I want to see it with entrée amongst the fine families of the kingdom. Thunder and damnation, we have got the money for it! All we need is the blood, and you are the means to that end. Oliver, you had best take me very seriously, indeed. You must know from your past experience that I am a man who means what he says and who says what he means."

"Sir, I must leave you now. We shall talk more about this later. At the moment I must make sure that the twins have indeed arrived here."

Mr. Grantford frowned. "Why, may I ask, must

you do it? Have they not someone to look after them?"

"They took a notion to run away, and we believe that they are headed for Woodhouse—"

Mr. Grantford smiled a sarcastic smile of triumph. "Well, what do you know! Even in London, with their sister a countess, they are still up to their old tricks. They prove my point to a period. Blood will tell, good or bad, and theirs is obviously not of the best."

"Oh, what is the use!" exclaimed Oliver, and he dashed out of the room.

It was nothing new to Oliver. These exchanges with his father had been going on for as long as he could remember and never once could he recall that he had ever come out of one with his point being gained. Many times he himself had been convinced that he had not had the right opinion of the facts to begin with; but, even when he was sure he was right, he came away from his parent feeling that he had not been. In the present case, he was not quite sure whether he was in the right or not. It was a complicated business, marriage and familial considerations. As he made his way out of the house onto the walk, his mind was taken up with the attempt to see his father's side of the question and how it might impinge upon his own interests.

He did not think to ride over to Bellflower Cottage. It never entered his mind, for the distance was a short walk along the road. It was a distance he had walked innumerable times and usually in the company of Percy.

There could be no question that his father had given him an awfully hard nut to crack. Cutting him off without a cent and he with no other means of support must bode poorly for any sort of comfortable married life—unless, of course, he was content to live upon the largesse of his wife's relations. In short, he would become a pensioner of Lord Dalby. He tried to believe that that was precisely the status that Percy was being accorded, but he could not convince himself. Even without his father, the viscount, Percy was independent, although modestly so. The post given him by Lord Dalby was no sinecure. Doing for one of the high justices of the nation called for something more than mere kinship. It galled him to think that Percy had stolen a march on him. If only his friend had confided in him about his ambitions, it might have started him thinking along such lines, so that he might have been able to offer his services to some politico as a secretary at this pass. As it was, he was completely unequipped to provide for a bride out of his own resources, and so it would be for a great number of years—perhaps forever, if his father stuck to his threat. That must be a most serious consideration for his attention.

Just how serious it was, he had to defer for the moment. He was arrived at the door of Bellflower Cottage. He knocked upon it, and shortly, it opened and Mrs. Sandringham stood before him, smiling a welcome.

"Dear Oliver, what a pleasant surprise! I have just received an express from Lord Dalby telling of the news—but how do you come to be here when everything is happening there—in London, of course? But do not stand there. Come in, come in and talk with me. I am dying to know all about it. Two engagements at the same time. Just leave it to my twins. I do not think they will ever do a thing by themselves except that they do it together."

She led him into the little parlor of the cottage and they sat down.

"Then I take it, Mrs. Sandringham, that neither Sophie nor Sarah has arrived yet?"

"No, they have not—but why should we expect them—and why are you here, Oliver?"

"I am sort of an advance party of one, madam. Lady Dalby and Percy are some hours behind me."

"And Sarah and Sophie, where are they?"

"I fear that that is something of a problem. We do not rightly know. It is her ladyship's opinion that they took it into their minds to run off to home, and we have been following their trail, as it were. That is, we were following right behind until it quite ran out somewhere after Linslade."

"Linslade? What on earth could they have to do at Linslade?"

"Well, that is what has us stumped. We thought that they might have gone another way at that point, but nothing suggested itself. It is possible that we overran them and they are behind us. They will arrive here eventually, you see."

"No, Oliver, I do not see! Why did they go off in

the first place, and what makes Pennie think that they would head for home?"

Oliver shook his head. "Nothing makes sense, Mrs. Sandringham. We had no reason to suspect that they were in any way unhappy with their prospects. Everything seemed to be on an even keel. Percy has received an appointment as clerk to his honor, Lord Dalby. The only fly in the ointment of our content is, perhaps, my father, with whom I have just concluded a most unhappy interview—"

"He is not happy with your engagement to Sophie?"

"No, decidedly not. He is out to defeat it at all costs."

"Disinherit you, I suppose."

Oliver nodded unhappily.

"How much of this does Sophie know or suspect?"

"Quite the whole of it. We were waiting for Lord Dalby to finish some work before he could sit down and have a talk with my governor, so Sophie was as aware of the problem as any of us."

"Well, for whatever it is worth, if I know my daughter, she will be showing up on your father's doorstep at any moment—and Sarah will not be far behind. Pennie is truly their sister and need never have doubted her instincts—but the delay does puzzle me. How do you think my girls are traveling?"

"Post chaise, for sure, Mrs. Sandringham."

"And you heard nothing to suggest that there had been an accident along the way?"

"Nothing like that."

"In that case, I presume that their vehicle suffered an inconvenience that took them off the road for a bit. They could have been laying over in any one of a number of inns while the vehicle was being put to rights. I shall not begin to worry yet. I have the feeling they will be here shortly. If there is one thing my twins know better than most females of any age, it is how to take care of themselves. They are very resourceful, you know."

"Indeed, I do know!" exclaimed Oliver with a smile of relief. "In that case, Mrs. Sandringham, I pray you will excuse me, for I still have the business of winning over my father to accomplish."

"Yes, you go right ahead, Oliver. I am sure you will succeed in the end. It is not conceivable that any father in his right mind could find the least thing exceptional in my Sophie—and you have been sweethearts since you were children. I was always sure of that. Good day to you, Oliver, and if the twins do show up, I'll send to you right away."

"Thank you, Mrs. Sandringham, and good day to you."

As he ambled back to his home, Oliver at first was pleased that Mrs. Sandringham was so very satisfied with him as a prospective husband to Sophie but then he had never expected any objections from that quarter. What did surprise him was how calmly Mrs. Sandringham took the news of his possible disinheritance. Surely, that prospect must dismay any bride's mother. It could be that she did not believe it could truly come to pass. Yes, that must be it! The loss of a fortune just could not be so easily dismissed.

He had to fault himself on that point. He had had a very good idea of his father's opinions regarding the female he might have to marry some day, so it had not been news to him, his father's hard-nosed attitude toward his engagement. Really, he should have thought longer and harder about the business instead of allowing himself to be rushed into it by Percy. Oh, yes, love was quite an important aspect of marriage, but it was not all. There was a practical side of things, and it was high time that he gave proper consideration to it. It was a very good idea of Percy's to have sent him on ahead. He had had the chance to open the discussion with the governor and he had not been eaten alive. There was still room for further discussion, and during it, he would have to think about his father's side of the matter. He had not done it before. He had let himself be blinded by his lifelong infatuation with Sophie. As a responsible adult, it was time he took himself in hand and examined this passion of his. Just how reasonable a thing was it, after all? Why, actually, he could not truly say at this pass whether or no it was Sophie or Sarah. Obviously there was the possibility that Sophie fell to him because Percy was truly enamored of Sarah. It went far to explain why Percy was able to recognize Sarah before ever he could be sure which twin was which. He was not so sure even now that he could do so without more than an occasional error.

Yes, he had got to think. Things might not be as they seemed, and if they were not, then he must know that before it was all too late. How awful to wind up a pauper and all for a wife he truly was not in love with. He had best have another talk with the governor. His thinking certainly was in need of clarification. Of that he was sure.

Chapter 11

There was no conversation amongst the riders as they made their way to the stables. There was a look of disappointment on Lord Leighton's face, and his eyes constantly traveled over to gaze upon Sophie.

Sophie kept her eyes upon the bridle path, her face masking her thoughts, and she kept her mount slightly forward of Sarah's.

Sarah had a look of concern on her face, and she attempted to make conversation. It proved impossible, however, because neither of her companions was in a mood to make any response.

When they arrived in the stable yard, Sophie did not wait for his lordship to assist her down but dismounted easily by herself while Sarah was being helped. Then, without waiting for her sister, she started off for the house.

Sarah would have followed, but his lordship detained her for a moment.

"Miss Sarah, I am at a loss for words to explain what has occurred. I pray you will make my apology to Miss Sophie. I should prefer to do it in person, but you see how it is."

"My lord, I will relay your message, but I would also point out, it is high time that my sister and I were on our way. I pray you will see to having the chaise brought to us as quickly as may be."

"As you wish, Miss Sarah. I shall see to it immediately."

Sarah turned and followed her sister to the house.

She did not catch up to her until they were in their chamber and then she found Sophie, crouched by the bed, weeping silently.

She came and sat on the floor beside her, taking her hand, and saying: "Sophie, I am sure you knew that something like that was going to happen. If you had not wanted it, you ought to have come with me to the stream."

Sophie clung to Sarah, crying: "Oh, what is wrong with me? Why does he affect me so?"

"Tell me, are you not truly in love with Oliver?"

"Well, you know that I am! Yet, I cannot stop thinking of John. Sarah, what is wrong with me?" she pleaded.

"I wish I knew. Lord Leighton is a most attractive gentleman, and I know that if I had not Percy,

I could be affected by him—but that is the point. I like him immensely, but I love Percy. Perhaps it is just the flattery inherent in his behavior to you. It is not I he is trying to devote himself to, it is you. I mean to say that that is bound to get in your way—I am sure it would have gotten in my way. Once we are away from Linscombe Park, everything will sort itself out quickly enough. I have asked his lordship to see to restoring the chaise to us. I do not think it would be at all wise for us to spend another night under his roof. If he took such a liberty with you this morning, it would be foolish to believe that even greater embarrassment would not be in store for you if we stayed on."

"But that is the trouble. I am not at all embarrassed. Sarah, I wanted him to kiss me and—and I would not mind if he wished to do it again!"

"But what of Oliver?"

"I just do not know! I never felt this way about Oliver. Sarah, what am I to do?"

"Oh, Sophie, this is awful! How are you going to be able to speak with Mr. Grantford when you are in this condition of uncertainty? After all, that is why we have come so far."

"Oh, I know, I know—and I feel so guilty about it."

"Come now. Dry your eyes. As soon as the chaise is ready, we must leave. You will be able to think more clearly when you are away from this place. I mean to say you have known Oliver for a lifetime and his lordship barely a day. Surely, it must say something to you."

"It does, it does, and there is no sense to it. If his lordship was to ask me to marry him right now, I could never refuse."

"Then there is no purpose in our staying one second longer. You are having a dream, sister dear. Lord Leighton is not about to propose to you on such short acquaintance. You would not have him if he did. Sophie, this is not like you. There is no sense to it. I pray you will not make a fool of yourself before his lordship. You have got to pull yourself together and think of tomorrow. You are betrothed, girl!"

Sophie took a deep breath. "Yes, you are right. I am behaving like a schoolgirl. One kiss and I am in paradise. It is nonsense. His lordship is handsome, and the spot was very romantic—in fact, there is an air about John that is something wistful, something tender, something sincere—"

"Sophie! Enough, I say! The next thing you know you will be making a comparison of him with Oliver!"

Sophie smiled shamefacedly and bit her lip. She chuckled as she nodded her head.

"Oh, dear!" exclaimed Sarah, softly, as she stared at her sister.

Neither of the girls experienced a desire to leave their room. A meeting with his lordship, as things stood, would be embarrassing for all parties, and so they remained seated in the chamber, conversing about what they ought to do. Sarah suggested that they be prepared to leave on the instant. Sophie agreed and they spent a few minutes gathering their things together.

Sarah picked up the make-do veil and wrinkled up her nose. "I suppose that we shall have to go on wearing this thing until we are home. After all, nothing has changed for us, has it? We still want no notice as we travel."

Said Sophie: "I almost regret that we ever came on this journey."

"But it was your idea. You felt that things were moving too slowly."

"Yes, I know—but, when you come to think about it, it was something for Oliver to do, not me. He might resent it. You saw with what disdain Lord Leighton listened to the business. It does seem to reflect upon Oliver, does it not?"

Sarah bit her lip and refrained from answering.

"Ah," continued Sophie, "you think so yourself."

"I cannot help it, dearest. I am sure that Percy, for all his slowness, would never have failed to face up to the problem—but I suppose that is not exactly fair, is it? Percy has neither the parent nor the dependence that Oliver suffers."

"Yes, but is it not strange that Oliver had never given thought to remedying the situation? Percy seems to have been thinking of his future, whereas Oliver gave no thought to it at all. He preferred to bask in the largesse of his father and borrow from Percy when he needed to."

"I pray you will leave me out of this discussion. Naturally I am heavily prejudiced in Percy's favor because I do love him. It is odd, isn't it, that when we were young, I felt a resentment toward Oliver for always leading Percy around? Perhaps that is what started my interest in him. But, today, Percy is a different sort entirely. I still do not think of him as being particularly fast in the upper story, but he does know what he wants and is bound to achieve it—and you know, I do think he is a most attractive gentleman even if he is not so very much taller than I am."

"That is the trouble! Sarah, the more I think on Oliver's qualities, the more I am at pains to determine what I see in him. True, he always seemed to lead Percy about by the nose, but no longer. In fact, he seems to me of late to be most unsure of himself."

"Would you have said this a day or so ago, before we ever arrived at Linscombe Park?"

"No, I admit it—but, perhaps, it is a good thing that it happened. It has made me think."

"Oh, Sophie, whatever you do, I pray you to be sure. You must not make comparisons with Lord Leighton. A kiss is not a proposal of marriage, as the novels would have us believe. Surely you are not so ingenuous as that."

"Yes, yes, I know," said Sophie, a little impatiently. "Still, I am thinking I would much rather stay on here a few more days than rush on up to Woodhouse for this chat with Mr. Grantford."

"You are beginning to sound like Oliver. Look you, once you have had your say with Mr. Grantford and he is won over, I have no doubt but that you will see everything in a far more favorable light than you do now. Mr. Grantford will be pleased, and Oliver will be like a new man for having this hurdle of his father's disapproving removed."

"I just do not feel very optimistic about Mr. Grantford—or Oliver, for that matter. What if Mr. Grantford says no to it and cannot be persuaded? Can Oliver persist in the face of his possibly being disinherited? What happens then?"

"It is not the end of the world, my love. I begin to wonder if your affection for Oliver is all that great. In any case, I do not see how that makes a difference. I mean to say, of course it makes a difference, but you are still quite young, and there is nothing to say that you have to get married because I am doing so. Just because we are twins has naught to say to it. We can always go back to London where there are plenty of suitors for your hand—and without me along all of the time, I dare say you will find it much easier with them. There is Lord Fallon. He was always fond of you and only lost patience because we did not help him to get to know which of us was which. It could be quite different another time."

Sophie slowly shook her head. "No . . . I do not think so . . . He does not compare to his lordship."

Sarah glanced at her sister, and there was frustration in her tones as she remarked: "Oh, what can be keeping the chaise!"

Finally, there came a knock upon their chamber door. A maid informed them that their post chaise was at the front door and awaited their pleasure.

She took up their things and followed them out of the room.

When they came into the reception hall, they found their host waiting for them. His face showed him to be under a strain, and his eyes sought out Sophie's.

She turned away and took a breath, leaving it to Sarah to say all that was necessary.

"My lord," said Sarah, "you have been more than kind. We cannot express how deep are our thanks to you and to her ladyship, the countess, for making us feel so much at home."

"Then may I prevail upon you to put off your departure until my lady mother can have a chance to say farewell. She will be heartbroken to discover that you have left. She was enchanted with your company and only went out this morning to pay a visit to a dear crony of hers who has not been feeling well lately. I am sure she will be returning at any minute."

Sophie grabbed at Sarah's sleeve and, as Sarah turned to her, gave a quick little shake to her head. His lordship saw it, and his face grew even more unhappy.

"My lord, we have lost so much time that we cannot afford to spare more. Our gladsome respects to the countess, and I pray that we may all of us meet again one day. Goodbye to you, my Lord Leighton."

The girls went out of the house and mounted up into the chaise that was standing by.

As they began to roll away, Sophie looked out of the window and saw his lordship standing by the door. He did not wave nor did she, but they stared at each other until the drive turned and descended a little, cutting off their sight of each other.

Sophie let out a deep sigh and sat back in her seat. "You were right, Sarah. It is better this way. Oliver has got to mean so much more to me than *any* man."

Sarah thought that it was an odd way of putting things but that she had better let it lie. She relapsed into silence and so did Sophie.

The chaise rolled on.

Chapter 12

When Lady Leighton returned home from her call, she inquired after her son and was informed that he awaited her in her sitting room. She repaired to it and discovered him pacing the floor.

"And how are our little dears?" she inquired brightly.

"Our little dears have quite flown the coop, my lady," he responded, looking up from his studying the floor.

He came over to her and took her by the hands, leading her to a small settee. They sat down and he said: "Mother, I do believe that you have a fool for a son."

"Well, that is not for you to say. Allow me to be the judge. Now, pray tell me why they are gone.

Could they not even stay long enough to say good-bye to me?"

"I dare say it was because I made it most uncomfortable for them to prolong their visit with us."

"Well, I imagine I had best hear all about it. Indeed, I am most sorry that we have lost their company. They are both of them so full of spirits and so very much alike, it is the most entertaining thing to see them together."

"It is surprising to me that you should say so. Of course I am aware that they are twins, but to me, they appear quite different. I could never mistake Sarah for Sophie."

"How very interesting. But what have you done that must make them flee with horror of you, my son?"

He smiled. "Never horror. Say rather distaste. I—er kissed Sophie while we were out for a ride this morning. Not quite the thing to do, wouldn't you say? After all, I am their host and to take such advantage. . . ." He shrugged in helplessness.

"She fought you?"

"Well, I would not have done it if she had. I am not a complete cad."

"I never thought that you were even a poorly finished one. May I inquire why you took the liberty? I know the both of them are quite fetching, but you have been with fetching females before and never managed to misbehave—or at least I never heard that you had—which is as good as saying that you never have. In fact, I am pleased as punch that you finally have, if you know what I mean."

"Well, at the moment it is not I whom we are discussing. I would—"

"But I thought it was. It is your so-called misbehavior that is the point of this discussion, and I should think it would be you, therefore, that we have got to speak about. Considering your past lack of interest in such sport, I am deeply curious to know why now and why this one."

"Is it not obvious? I have fallen in love with her."

"Yes, I thought you had—and I am extremely disappointed that you were so easily defeated. I thought she would have made a most excellent partner. By the way, how is her seat?"

"She sits a horse as well as one could ask. They both of them are superb horsewomen. They take to it so naturally and easy, it was a pleasure to observe them."

"Then, perhaps you will tell me why you let the one get away."

"How could I stop them? She is gone to ask for the hand of her Oliver from his father. What could I do or say in the face of that?"

"Well, you did start, and as I have not heard that she made any objection, I am hard put to understand why you saw fit to leave it at that."

"In broad daylight?"

"You have a tongue, have you not? You know the girl's language, do you not? You could have spoken to her, could you have not? Really, John, at your age you ought to know better than that. Here, I was sure that I had finally got me a most excellent daughter-in-law. It has been too lonely on the estate by far for me. Now, why pray are you standing so idly about?"

"Dammit all, because I have not the heart to do anything else. She is gone and there's an end to it."

"I wonder if all mothers have as much trouble with their grown sons as I do with mine! If you love the girl, you will never win her, she on the road to Leicester and you here in Linscombe."

"Oh, really, Mother! Am I to go after her like 'young Lochinvar come out of the east'?"

"He came out of the west."

"Whatever."

"Do you think she is in love with this Oliver, my lord?"

"I assume she must be if she is going to all that trouble for him with his father."

"You assume so, but you are not sure."

"That is what I said, my lady."

"Then why do you not go after her and make sure?"

"Because it would not be at all fitting. It would be an intrusion into her private affairs. I am sure I would not be welcome."

The countess regarded her son with disdainful disappointment. "As to the welcome, you cannot be sure until you try. As to the intrusion into her private affairs, well, I should hope so. How else is the business to be conducted?"

"But she has already plighted her troth to the fellow," his lordship pointed out and then held his breath for his mother's rebuttal.

"You can not even be sure of that, my lord. In cases of this sort, a female's word is never to be trusted—and I am not about to explain it to you. You have been married and must know something. But I shall not belabor these points. I shall only go so far as to point out how lacking in your duty as a host you are to allow two young ladies to go out upon the open road, completely unprotected."

Lord Leighton stood up. He was grinning now. He came over to his mother and planted a kiss upon her forehead. Stepping back, he executed a little bow to her. "My lady, I knew you would find a way to let me go after them without making an utter cake of myself. I thank you."

"The way to thank me is to bring me back that young lady to be my daughter-in-law. I have taken quite a fancy to her."

"Indeed, how very convenient, for so have I. Well, I must be running off. I am sure you will excuse me."

"I pray you will cease your jawing, my lord, and get on with it."

"To hear is to obey, mother mine," he said with a chuckle. Turning on his heel, he walked quickly out of the room.

Lord Leighton came racing through the gates of his estate and out onto the road. He wheeled his horse about and shot off in the direction the post chaise had taken. His charge lasted a quarter of a mile. It took that long for his good sense to overcome his impetuosity. A tug on the reins brought the gallop to an end, and he set his mount into an easy canter that would not wear out the beast, yet would bring him up to the chaise reasonably soon despite its speed of travel. All he had to do was to go cross-country and he could get ahead of the vehicle before ever it reached Bletchley.

Twenty minutes later, he came out onto the high road a mile or two below Bletchley and sat his horse, patiently waiting for the chaise to make its appearance.

As the chaise rolled through Soulbury on its way to meet with the high road at Stoke Hammond, Sophie sniffed and said: "We ought to have waited to say goodbye to her ladyship."

Sarah turned from the window and regarded her sister for a moment. She saw a tear trickle down Sophie's cheek and she was disturbed.

"My dear, I thought it best that we not tarry. For as long as you remained in his presence, your thinking was bound to be muddled."

Another tear trickled down Sophie's cheek, followed by a sigh so deep it was almost a sob.

"Goodness gracious, Sophie, whatever is the matter?" exclaimed Sarah.

"I am feeling quite miserable. Do you object? Surely there is no law against my feeling miserable, is there?"

"Well, you do not have to snap my head off. I see that you are and I marvel at it. One kiss and it is bellows to mend with your heart? Sophie, I pray you be sensible or you will make fools of both of us. Think on it. Here you are about to call upon Mr. Grantford, yet you seem to be full of Lord Leighton. Now how can you in all conscience stand before Mr. Grantford and make your plea?"

"I know that!" wailed Sophie. "And that is precisely what is making me miserable!"

"Oh, I wish we never accepted his lordship's invitation! If you continue in this fashion, the entire trip will be for naught, and we shall be made to look a proper pair of silly geese."

"Oh, I know that, too—but what am I to do?"

"Think of Oliver."

"I am trying to—but it is his lordship who always comes between."

Sarah sat back in her seat feeling quite defeated. "Then perhaps we might as well turn the .chaise about and go back to London."

"Perhaps. I don't know!"

"As it happens, we cannot do so. We have not the funds. We shall barely have sufficient to get to Woodhouse."

"Then we have no choice but to continue."

"Well, are you going to speak with Mr. Grantford when you get there?"

"I really do not have any choice, do I? I am sure that Oliver would be brokenhearted if I did not."

"Since I believe that you are in love with him, you might as well go on with it, of course—but, as Oliver has not the vaguest idea of what we are about, I do not see that your failure to broach the subject of your marriage with Mr. Grantford can affect him one way or the other."

"That is true—yet, I feel that I must. Oliver and I are promised, and that must take precedence over every other consideration."

"I think so."

"So then why must I feel so awfully blue about it?"

"It is possible that if Oliver were here with us right this moment, you would not feel down in the dumps at all."

Sophie took a deep breath and sat up. "I am sure you are right, dear. I am sure that by the time we arrive in Woodhouse, I shall be feeling much better and quite up to meeting with Mr. Grantford, too."

"Ah, that is so much better."

The chaise came to a pause before entering onto the high road and then made its way onto it, now headed directly for Bletchley.

Said Sarah: "I hope you mean what you say, my dear."

"I do," said Sophie, firmly. "I am quite resolved to it, and nothing can change my mind."

Sarah had been looking ahead, out of the front window. Beyond the post boy, seated on the lead horse, she could make out a lone rider standing by the side of the road. Her heart sank as she turned to her sister.

"Sophie, love, I do hope you mean what you say, for if I am not mistaken, I do believe that we are about to meet with Lord Leighton once again. See, there he is, and I'll wager it is this chaise he has been waiting for. He must have cut cross-country and ridden like the wind to have got so far ahead of us so soon."

Sophie took one look and let out a groan, falling back into her seat as she sent a pleading look for help to her sister.

Sarah saw his lordship raise his hand to stop the chaise, and the post boy, recognizing him, began to draw back on the reins. As the chaise slowly rolled to a stop, Sarah hissed. "Remember your resolve! Now sit up and and look as though butter would not melt in your mouth!"

Sophie, realizing that that was truly all she could do, obeyed.

When his lordship came to open the door to converse with them, he discovered two very well collected and charming ladies so pleased to meet with him once again.

For a moment he stood uncertain, his hand still on the open door.

"My lord, what a delightful surprise!" exclaimed Sophie, smiling up at him.

Her smile appeared to restore some order to his soul, and he smiled back as he made a sweeping bow.

"Ladies, I have come to offer my most abject apologies for being so remiss in my duties as your host. I am come to make amends. I do not know what I was thinking to allow ladies, who had been under my roof, to go forth onto the public roads, completely unprotected. To show you the sincerity of my repentance, instead of furnishing you with a pair of footmen to see you safe, I have elected to accompany you myself to your journey's end. I humbly pray you will allow it."

Said Sarah, quickly: "My lord, you are too kind, and it would be monstrous of us to put you to such trouble. We have come this far from London in such security and comfort as to require no such sacrifice on your part."

"But, if my lord believes that there are unknown perils lying before us," added Sophie, gaining a black look from Sarah in the process, "we cannot help but be grateful for your company."

"Excellent! Then it is settled. I shall bear all charges, since you are, in effect, still my guests. By your leave, ladies, I shall hitch my horse to the chaise and join you."

Sarah knew she was outvoted by Sophie's smile of pleasure and decided to put a good face on it.

Lord Leighton quickly tied his horse to the back of the carriage and came to take his seat between them in the vehicle. He called out to the driver, and the chaise started up again with a very cheerful post boy on the leader. He was bound to get a far greater gratuity now that this rich lord had joined the party than ever he could have expected from two females no matter what their rank and wealth.

Chapter 13

"Jepperson, where the devil is that brief I was studying?" demanded Lord Dalby from behind his desk.

Without a word, the butler stepped up to the desk, raised up a packet of documents from under which he retrieved a set of papers which he handed to the earl.

"Now what blamed fool put them there!"

"I wish you would not put it that way, your lordship."

Lord Dalby grinned. "I did, didn't I?"

Jepperson allowed himself the smallest smile and nodded slightly.

"I need a clerk, Jepperson. That is my trouble. Can you imagine it? I am a judge of the King's

Bench Court and I have not yet got me a clerk. It is those blasted, blessed in-laws of mine. Egad, but I shall be glad to get them married off! Then, perhaps, I shall have me my clerk and I shall have me my wife once again. Here I have been wed—how many months has it been, Jepperson?"

"A trifle more than three months, your lordship."

"Precisely so, and already I am bereft of in-laws, guests and wife. I do not mind the loss of the former two, but the latter has come to mean quite a bit, you know."

"I am sure the entire household misses the countess, your lordship."

"Well, thanks to you, everything appears to be quite shipshape in her absence."

"Your lordship, she has been gone but twenty-four hours."

"So little as that? It seems like weeks to me. I do not think I shall be able to stand much more of it. I mean to say we are still newlyweds."

"Yes, your lordship."

"Oh, stop grinning and act your age, fellow!" exclaimed the earl with a laugh.

He stared down at the brief in his hands, and Jepperson made a move to retire.

"Stay, old fellow. Stay a bit," said Lord Dalby, holding up his hand, his other laying down the papers. "Has there been any word at all from the countess?"

"No, your lordship, but even if she had sent an express on her arrival, I am sure we could not expect to receive it until late tonight."

"Yes, you are right. But the thing of it is I cannot begin to think about briefs and arguments in her absence. Now, isn't that strange? I have been a bachelor all of my life and never had the least difficulty applying myself before this. Strange the power a female can exert over a chap. Now, mind you, I am not complaining a bit, not one bit—but it is playing hob with my concentration in the courtroom—and this blasted case is only just beginning. Well, I shall just have to rule myself incompetent for the time being and have another of my colleagues take over for me. I am going home to Beaumanor and Lady Dalby. Care to come along with me?"

"Oh, I should be delighted to see the old place once again, your lordship," exclaimed the old butler, showing a beaming smile.

"Indeed, I thought that would get a rise out of you, you old iron-faced fraud! Come along, then. Get things ready for a fast run, while I go to court and arrange for another judge to replace me. I am bound to return with a clerk and a wife, if God wills it—and I pray that He does!"

When his lordship returned home, it was not quite noon on the day after Lady Dalby had departed for Woodhouse. Jepperson was attired in the togs of a Leicestershire huntsman and was standing ready for him with two large steeds that were broad-chested and powerful. Obviously the horses were bred hunters.

At a glance his lordship was impressed and smiled at Jepperson. He remarked: "Well, you have not forgotten your old duties, I see. Yes, an excellent choice, Jepperson. We shall not be held to the roads but can go cross-country whenever it will save us time. Those two are obviously from the Beaumanor stables. What ever made you think to bring hunters into the city, old chap?"

"They make excellent saddle horses and are available for just this sort of emergency, my lord."

"And your point is proved by the very circumstances, isn't it? Well, this will be like a chase to rival all chases. Do you think that they can make the distance without change?"

"I know these two, your lordship. They will go a steady nine miles an hour and twice the distance of any team you can name. It is something over a hundred miles we have to cover. With one or two layovers of about an hour each, I'll give odds that we will be in Woodhouse a little after midnight."

His lordship frowned. "That sounds like a brag to me. We can hardly drive the poor beasts through the dark, you know."

"What I mean to say is that it is a hundred or so miles by road, I am sure we can save at least twenty of them, your lordship."

"Well, we shall see. I shall be more than happy if we can greet tomorrow's sun at Beaumanor. Let me change into a habit and we are off."

"I have had your things laid out, your lordship."

"Excellent. I shall only be a moment."

Lady Dalby was feeling very weary. It had been such a long, hard ride from London to Leicestershire. They had not stopped more than a few times, and upon this, the very next day, her weariness was exacerbated by the disappointment and worry occasioned by the absence of her sisters. It was over time that they should have arrived if Woodhouse had been their destination. Her mind was too beclouded to think clearly, and she missed her lord with a passion, not only his presence but his sagacity. She felt that she could no longer cope with the situation and must have him close to help her through this trying time.

She was seated at her old writing table in Bellflower Cottage trying to compose a letter to him, one that would not unduly worry him yet bring him without delay to her side. Actually she had a wish to weep, and a few tears did escape to bespatter her letter, so that she had to tear it up and start over again. Oh, where, oh, where were the twins?

Oliver was with his father, and she thought that a good thing. Perhaps, some troubles in that direction might be avoided as a result of the father and son chats that must occur. In any case, with Alan out here, he could take a hand in it. She was sure that he, of any one, could convince the intransigent Mr. Grantford not to stand in the way of the children's happiness.

Percy had proved himself a veritable jewel. He had been most thoughtful and considerate throughout the trip. He had insisted upon staying with her during her vigil, but she had preferred to be alone and sent him off to inform his parents about his decision to wed Sarah. She did not expect any trouble on that score from the viscount.

She finally finished a letter that she was not too satisfied with, but it was a distinct improvement over her earlier efforts, and time was passing. She would have it sent express, and Alan would have it by the next morning. Oh, dear, after that she would have to be waiting for Alan to appear as well as for the twins!

She sent a girl off to Mountsorrel to arrange for the letter to be transferred to the London stage, and sat back with a pot of tea, trying to understand how she could have missed out on reckoning the twins' destination.

Percy came to call upon her, and she received him in the parlor of the cottage.

"How did your parents take the news, Percy?" she inquired after asking him to join her in a cup.

He took a sip and nodded his head. "Quite well, thank you. The viscount was quite pleased of the notice that Lord Dalby has taken of me and said it was sure to keep me out of trouble." He smiled apologetically. "As to what he had to say about Sarah as my bride"—his cheeks turned pink—"I am afraid I dare not repeat his remarks in delicate company, my lady, but I assure you it was enthusiastic, to say the least."

Lady Dalby let out a little chuckle. "Yes, your father always had an eye for a face and a figure."

Percy's face turned scarlet. "Oh, I say!" he murmured.

"Well, I am pleased to learn that Sarah is getting a father-in-law who appreciates her."

Percy had to clear his throat, and he rushed to change the subject. "I fear that all is not going so well at the Grantfords. I passed by their place and saw Oliver standing by the gate with a long face. He informed me that he had been thinking, that his father and he had been having chats. I think rather arguments, and from Oliver's phiz he was not getting the best of it by far."

"I am so sorry to hear it. I have just sent an express to my husband asking him to come out. I am sure he will have something to say to Mr. Grantford that will turn the tide for Oliver."

"But there is the rub, I think. I am beginning to wonder if Oliver, instead of wishing the tide to turn, is not going along with it."

"Oh, surely you are mistaken, Percy. He cannot have such a wish. I am sure he adores Sophie."

"I have always thought so, too; but, if you heard him muttering things about what his father had said to him and how the old gentleman truly had something on his side of the question—well, I am not so sure that Oliver quite knows what he wants to do. I believe he is having doubts and I cannot imagine why he should. After all, Sarah and Sophie are so very lovable, I cannot imagine what Mr. Grantford could say to him that could count against the match. Can you, my lady?"

Lady Dalby raised a hand to her troubled brow. "Percy, everything is so at sixes-and-sevens that I do not know where I am at. First, we have got to find the twins. Then, and only then, can we begin to worry about Oliver and his problem with his father."

"Quite, my lady. I had only hoped to take our thoughts from what, of course, must be our first concern."

"Thank you, Percy, it is quite noble of you."

"Well, I shall not intrude further, my lady. My respects to Mrs. Sandringham."

"Percy, I pray you will not leave. Why do you not join my mother and me at dinner? We should love to have your company."

He nodded and smiled ruefully. " 'Misery loves company,' isn't it? Thank you, my lady. I should be honored."

It was dusk as the chaise approached Wigston, a few miles south of the city of Leicester.

"We shall be coming to Leicester shortly," said Lord Leighton, looking out of the window.

"Yes," said Sarah. "In a few short hours we shall be home."

Sophie merely nodded.

Conversation was at a low ebb in the chaise. By this time, all the usual topics had been exhausted, and neither Lord Leighton nor Sophie appeared to be in a mood to talk—which was a wonder. For right from the moment that his lordship had joined the ladies, both he and Sophie had been going at it as though a silence would have been an offense.

Sophie was doing her best to indicate, without saying as much, that despite anything that had occurred between them in the past, she aimed to be friendly. For his part, his lordship was out to determine if the offense he had given was altogether unforgivable. As it became apparent to the two that a strong liking remained between them, the conversation had grown quite lively, and Sarah had been amused and had joined in. But, once all innocuous subjects had been exhausted, only the intimate remained, and neither his lordship nor Sophie dared to tread in such delicate areas. Sarah's presence was discouragement enough to Sophie, and as for his lordship, he had the added uneasiness arising from the fact that he believed that he had no right to be there. Miss Sophie was an engaged female, and he was an honorable gentleman. As long as he stayed with the ladies in his role as protector, his conscience could remain at ease. Unfortunately, it was not the same for his heart. Sitting so close to Sophie, wanting her more and more with each passing mile, he began to experience trouble keeping his end of the talking blandly pleasant. Somehow he had got to take Sophie aside and make the state of his affections plain to her. He would worry about apologies to Oliver Grantford another time.

A strange sound penetrated into his mind and put all of this thinking to flight. He excused himself to the ladies, leaned forward and slipped the windscreen open and shouted to the post boy, over the backs of the team: "Hoy! Stop the rig! At once, do you hear?!"

The post boy brought the carriage to a halt and

turned about in the saddle to see what was the trouble.

"There is a strange noise coming from the new wheel. You had better have a look at it."

"Yes, your lordship. At once, your lordship."

The post boy hobbled the two lead horses and went back to examine the new wheel. He came back to the front of the carriage, ducked his head at the earl and said: "A thousing apologies, your lordship, but the leather has dropped off an' the hub be as dry as a bone. We cannot travel far without we shall be losin' the wheel, for you see how it is—" He stood at ease and began to explain, but the earl cut him short.

"Yes, I understand how it is. Can you get us as far as a decent inn?"

"The Stag and Pheasant be a nice place, your lordship, an' I can have the wheel all set to go first thing in the mornin'."

"Very well. Take us there. As for tomorrow's plans, I shall let you know. Now drive slowly, or you will burn off the axle."

"Indeed, your lordship," replied the post boy, trying to mask his indignation at the uncalled-for advice.

The post boy remounted and started the chaise off at a very slow walk.

Lord Leighton sat back and remarked to the ladies with a chuckle: "This chaise seems to be a hard-luck rig. I do not think we shall be able to proceed in it tomorrow. What I would like to suggest is that I hire us a pair of horses and we finish the journey in the saddle—or is Woodhouse too far for a lady to ride?"

Said Sarah: "Truly, my lord, we are practically home now. It is not as much as a dozen miles and we can easily do it tonight by dinner time."

"Oh, no, Sarah!" protested Sophie. "I do not think that we dare chance it. I am sure that the roads are not all that good. Besides, my lord is not acquainted with the route and could easily come a cropper in the dark. It is best we lay over and finish the journey in the morning. Why, we can be at Beaumanor for breakfast and after a delightful morning's ride, I am sure."

"That sounds excellent advice, Miss Sarah," said his lordship. "Riding in the dark can be particularly hazardous when one is unfamiliar with the road."

He said it with an ingratiating smile, and Sarah gave it up. After all, Percy was away off in London, and rushing on to Woodhouse could not make any difference to her.

Chapter 14

The Stag and Pheasant was an undistinguished hostelry of ancient vintage but adequate accommodation. As the twins were well known in Leicester, so close to their home, not only for their remarkable resemblance to each other but as the daughters of his honor, Judge Sandringham, there would have been not the slightest difficulty in obtaining rooms. But, now that they were sisters-in-law to the earl of Dalby, they could command even greater deference. Upon learning that it was the earl of Leighton who was their escort, the innkeeper could not help but believe that he was entertaining a future countess as well, and the entire inn was put at their disposal.

They retired to their rooms to remove the stains

of travel and get ready for a meal before retiring for the night. It was agreed that they would start for Woodhouse very early in the morning and could use a good night's rest.

Lord Leighton parted with the twins at the door to their room, saying that he would call for them in an hour if that was all right. It was, and the twins went into their chamber.

As they busied themselves, Sarah asked: "Pray tell me, sister dear, precisely what you intend to do with the earl of Leighton once you have got him to Beaumanor."

"Sarah, you are being particularly nasty. You know very well that I had nothing to do with his lordship's coming after us."

"Well, I am sure he did not come after *me!* And the way you practically threw yourself at him, he cannot help but think you are interested in him more than is seemly in a girl who is pledged to another gentleman."

"I did no such thing. I was merely filling in with conversation that a loving sister of mine would have little to do with. What did you expect? There was Lord Leighton along with us and being rather charming, you must admit. If I did not respond to his chatting, who would?"

"Really, it was never that bad. I am sure I held up my end of it. Sophie, do you realize that his lordship is going all the way home with us and he is an earl? There is no one at Beaumanor, and we do not even know if Mama is at home in Bellflower Cottage. Whatever in the world are we to do with him once we are there? We are two lone females. We can hardly put him up with us."

"Well, we can hardly say to him: 'Thank you, my lord, you have been too kind. Now, we must say farewell. Kindly turn your horse about and return you to Linscombe Park.' "

"I agree, and it is exactly what I am trying to point out to you. We have got to say goodbye to my lord here at the inn. We are perfectly capable of riding those twelve miles by ourselves. We have done it more than a few times before."

"Oh, Sarah, have you no appreciation in you for his kindness to us? Surely, we are bound to show him all the hospitality that is within our power."

"But we cannot have him under the same roof with us and no chaperone!"

"Exactly—but you forget we have two roofs at our disposal. We can certainly put him up at our sister's place next door—Beaumanor—while we stay at Bellflower Cottage. What could be more simple than that?"

Sarah sniffed. "I hope, then, that you will be very happy as you go to call upon Mr. Grantford, knowing that you have his lordship to speak to upon your return."

Sophie sniffed. "I do not know as I shall speak to Mr. Grantford after all. It *is* for Oliver to do that, as everybody will admit."

"Oh, I am so sorry I ever came along on this trip with you!"

"I am sorry, too! Please recall that I did not ask you to come with me."

"No, but you were mighty happy that I did—until we ended up in Linscombe Park, that is."

"Well, surely, you are not going to blame me for that. You never objected to it, as I recall."

Sarah stared at her sister for a moment. Then she shook her head and came over to her. "Sophie, have you fallen out of love with Oliver in favor of Lord Leighton?"

Sophie threw herself into Sarah's arms, tears trickling down her cheeks. "Oh, Sarah, I do not know!"

Sarah patted her, comfortingly, on her shoulder, and said: "Oh, if only Oliver were about, we should soon see all of this sorted out."

"Yes, if only Oliver were about. If Oliver had come out to his father in the first place, not any of this would have occurred. I should never ha-have m-met J-John!"

The thought was too sad to bear. She began to weep anew.

Said Sarah: "Oh, I shall be so glad when tomorrow is over! At least then we shall all know what is in your mind. I mean to say it was all so very simple when there was only Oliver. Pray tell me this, love, how does Lord Leighton feel about you?"

"H-he k-kissed me!"

"I am quite aware of it—but did he declare himself to you before—or after?"

Sophie shook her head "He just stared at me."

Sarah shrugged. "I do not know what to say. It is so different from how it was with Percy and me."

"I can assure you it is quite different from how it was with Oliver and me."

"Well, may I suggest we leave it for a bit? We have got to dine with his lordship this evening, and there is nothing to be gained by going on in this fashion."

Sophie nodded, dried her eyes and the two sisters helped each other to change.

Lord Leighton had arranged for a private room in which they could sample the best of what the Stag and Pheasant could offer in the way of dinner. It was plain fare but fresh, prepared without recourse to exotic herbs and spices. But the travelers were famished, and their appetite was sufficient sauce to encourage them to do justice to the repast. Eating also did away with the necessity for conversation, which all of them seemed pleased to forgo.

After it was done, his lordship saw the ladies back to their chambers and then came back down to commune with a bottle of port before retiring. He was not too happy about things in general, feeling frustrated in his wish to get closer to Sophie. The fact that Sarah was always by made him uneasy. He did not feel that she was his friend, and her presence acted as a damper on his wit. He was sure that if she had proved more congenial, he could have mildly flirted with Sophie and thus been able to establish some sort of mutual feeling between them, however slight. He knew *her* to be a friend. The way she looked at him told him that much. There was something warm in her glances to him, but he could not be sure if they had any greater meaning. The kiss had certainly not solved anything. She had not repulsed him. He suspected that she might have enjoyed it. He hoped so—but he could not be sure about that either. He had so lost himself in that moment of passion, he was sure he could have believed anything he wanted to believe with regard to how she might have felt about him at that moment. If only he could get her away from her sister for just a moment or two!

Glancing at the bottle from which he had been pouring liberal sips, he was startled to see the level so low. He put down his tumbler and frowned. He needed no bottled courage at this moment. He was determined to see Sophie by herself and he would have to make the request even at the risk of her refusal. He pushed himself back from the table and got up. Straightening out his clothes, he stood erect and strode out of the little dining room.

At the twins' door, he lightly knocked.

"Yes, who is it?" he heard Sarah respond.

"It is I, John," he said.

He heard someone coming to the door and bit his lip. If it was Sarah, things would be damned difficult.

The door opened and Sophie peered out, a smile on her face: "Yes, my lord?"

He felt at ease immediately and smiled down at her. "Miss Sophie, I have a need to speak with you—in private. You could do me the greatest favor if you would step out into the corridor, here, for a bit. I shan't keep you long."

There was a quizzical look in Sophie's eyes as she gave his request a moment's thought. Then she nodded and turned to say to Sarah, "I shall be just outside the door with his lordship for a moment, Sarah," and came out to join him, leaving Sarah frowning.

"Yes, my lord? What is it you wish to say?"

"First I must beg your pardon for having to come to you like this, but cooped up in the chaise as we were, all three of us, there was no opportunity to speak—and, here in the inn, it has been devilishly difficult because Sarah is always about. If I had the least suspicion that she favored me in any way, I should not have been so hesitant, but I sense that she does not, for some reason, approve of me and, therefore, I can hardly speak my mind with regard to you in her presence."

Sophie nodded understandingly and waited for him to proceed.

"The thing of it is that I must explain to you that I am not given to taking advantage of young ladies who are defenseless and under my roof. It is not a thing I could ever countenance, and so, what occurred between us on the ride this morning, I pray you will believe was a gesture of the most sincere."

"Sincere, my lord? I am not sure that I understand," she replied calmly.

He hesitated, feeling not the least encouraged by her demeanor.

Sophie, on the other hand was experiencing a

palpitation of the heart that threatened to undo her completely if he did not get on with it.

He took a deep breath and said: "Miss Sophie, what I mean to say is that it was beyond my powers to resist the temptation, for, indeed, I am in love with you!" he ended hoarsely.

Sophie's heart gave a bound, and her pulses began to race as she stood there, gazing up into his face all starry-eyed.

Once again Lord Leighton discovered that he could not resist temptation, and folded her into his arms, completely unmindful of two travelers who had just mounted up to the floor and were coming down the corridor.

Sophie, too, was completely absorbed in what his lordship was about to do and she did not struggle the least bit but raised her lips to meet his.

"What in the bloody blue blazes is this?!" cried a voice harshly, just behind them, and they leaped apart, looking very guilty, his lordship's face quite pale with anger at the interruption, while Sophie's face, a picture of shock and embarrassment, stared at the intruder unable to say a word.

"Sophie, how can you do this thing, and who is this scurrilous bounder? Dammit, fellow, speak and identify yourself that I may know what base cur I have got to deal with!——and I demand to know what you have done with her sister!"

Now, great fear filled Sophie's breast, but before she could intervene, Lord Leighton drew himself up and retorted: "And who in bloody blazes are you, fellow, to come poking your nose in what cannot be any of your business!"

"Oh, Alan, no! Let me explain!" cried Sophie, throwing herself between the two men.

At that point, the door opened, and Sarah put out her head. Seeing Lord Dalby, she smiled and cried out, joyfully: "Alan! How marvelous! Were you seeking us?"

Immediately Lord Leighton bowed to Lord Dalby: "My lord, I beg your pardon. Had I known it was you, I would have never turned on you so. I crave forgiveness for my insolence, Lord Dalby."

His lordship appeared taken aback, but his anger remained. "I do not understand how you come to know me, for I do not know you, sir. But, then, you must know that this lady is my sister-in-law, the sister of my countess, and under my protection. Your conduct, sir, if that is the case, is doubly reprehensible, and I demand an explanation."

"My lord, I have the honor to be John, earl of Leighton, your humble servant and I shall be pleased to make all explanations that you may require—but not out here in this public way. If we could retire to a more private place, my lord?"

"Alan, what is going on? Sophie, for heaven's sake, what have you done?" demanded Sarah.

Lord Dalby turned to the twins. "Ladies, I must get to the bottom of this. I pray his lordship and I may use your chamber for our discussion."

Said Sarah: "You had better, or I should never forgive either of you. I wish to hear what this is all about, too!"

Lord Dalby turned to Lord Leighton and said: "After you, my Lord Leighton."

"Thank you, my Lord Dalby," replied Lord Leighton as he followed Sarah and Sophie back into the room.

Lord Dalby closed the door and stood in front of it waiting, his hands folded across his chest, taking Lord Leighton's measure. His pose was completely destroyed by a knock on the door. He had to unfold his arms, step back and open it.

It was Jepperson, loaded down with luggage. "Is there any change of plans, your lordship?"

His lordship raised a hand to his troubled brow and replied: "Damn and blast! I am not at all sure. Wait in the room for me, but do not unpack—I say, it is not all that far to Woodhouse. The horses are not so spent that you could not run up there and inform her ladyship that her sisters have been found—and tell her where we are. I do not intend to stir from this place until I have come to an understanding of what is going on. Of course, you are not to say anything of the sort to Lady Dalby, you understand. Merely tell her where we are and be guided by her wishes."

"Very good, your lordship. It is an easy ride, one that I am quite familiar with."

Lord Dalby closed the door and turned to the occupants of the room. Lord Leighton stepped forward to speak.

Lord Dalby raised an authoritative hand to silence him and said: "Your turn will come later, my lord. I have a wish to speak with my relations

first. They have a bit of explaining to do to me first.
Young ladies, I am highly wroth with you. Have
you any idea of the consternation, the worry, the
anxiety to which you put your sister? Have you any
idea of the anxiety that you caused your fiancés?
What manner of lark could have been so important
that, without a word to any of those who so dearly
love you, you eloped out onto the public roads,
completely unprotected, a possible prey to any thief
or rogue"—here, he conferred a scathing glance at
Lord Leighton—"who happened to come along?
This little escapade has had consequences that
reach far beyond your immediate family. I have
had to disqualify myself from my duties at King's
Bench Court to come out looking for you. All this
just for a prank? By heaven, I had thought you had
outgrown all such childish nonsense! When you
were young, it was quite the most amusing thing to
observe, but now that you are women grown, even
upon the eve of your marriages, it is shameful in
the extreme. Tell me, when shall all this outrageous
behavior cease?"

Said Sarah: "It is your tale, Sophie. You tell
him."

Sophie made a face and looked to Lord
Leighton. He was puzzled at her glance.

Said Lord Dalby: "You need not look to the
gentleman. He has nothing to say to this. I would
hear what you have to say and I am waiting, young
lady. What possible excuse can you offer for having
run away from us?"

Sophie bit her lip, looked at Lord Leighton once

more, took a deep breath and declared: "It was all Oliver's fault!"

"That is not even a poor beginning! Poor Oliver was quite out of his mind with concern—as was Percy, Miss *Sarah* Sandringham! Tell me, do you never consider for one moment the feelings of those who love you?"

"But I tell you, Alan, it *was* Oliver's fault!" insisted Sophie. "He was content to sit about and wait for you to intervene with Mr. Grantford. Well, I was not! I decided to take matters into my own hands. Knowing that neither you nor Pennie would allow it, I knew that I dare not even hint of my plans to you. I did not even inform Sarah of my intentions—so you have no call to blame her. When she saw what I was up to, she decided that she had better come along with me—"

"She ought to have dissuaded you, by God!"

"Well, she tried. I tell you truly she tried—but, when she understood the depth of my determination, she knew she could never sway me from my purpose."

"Purpose? What was your purpose in all of this? Merely to run away because things were not moving fast enough to suit you?"

"Well, of course not! I proposed to speak with Mr. Grantford myself. I was sure that I could convince him that our love must be the first consideration—oh, dear!" She broke off and looked at Lord Leighton, apologetically.

He was looking a bit pale.

"So that is your intention, is it?" retorted Lord

Dalby. "Have you not the least notion of how embarrassing such an outrageous conversation must be to Mr. Grantford? Do you think that only love is under consideration when it comes to marriage?"

"Well, that is all that should matter!" retorted Sophie. "You are the last to say otherwise, my lord!"

"And just what do you mean by that remark, young lady?" asked Lord Dalby, beginning to fume.

"You can hardly claim that *your* bride brought you any advantage. As I recall, the marriage settlements were quite one-sided."

Lord Dalby shot an embarrassed glance at Lord Leighton, who stood fascinated with the interchange.

He shot back: "Now that will be quite enough, young lady! It is not your sister's marriage we are discussing at the moment but yours. In fact, I do not see that we have any need to discuss even that any further. Thanks to your escapade, I am now on the scene, and there is no need for you to have to beard Mr. Grantford in his lair. *I* shall do the honors. It is what you wished, is it not?"

Sophie bit her lip and hesitated.

"Oh, come, now! I pray you will not turn contrary. There is nothing to be gained by it. Oliver is at Woodhouse—"

"He is?" gasped Sophie, turning pale.

"Yes, he is, and so is your sister, and, my dear Sarah, Percy is there, too. I suspect that once Jepperson has delivered my message, we shall have the entire crowd descend upon us. Actually, you should be punished, but I dare say that we all are so relieved to find you safe—and in the nick of time if I had my guess—" he added, glancing balefully at Lord Leighton, "it will be a joyful reunion. Now, be at ease. I shall be speaking with Mr. Grantford on the morrow and am sure to win him over."

He turned to Lord Leighton. "It is your turn, my lord. I am now prepared to listen to a defense of your conduct. I warn you I am lawyer and judge and come well prepared to render a verdict."

Lord Leighton's lips were tight with tension as he stared at Lord Dalby for a moment before he responded. "My lord, as I have listened to your comments these past minutes, I have been made to realize that my conduct is indeed indefensible. I must plead guilty to having made advances to a lady, betrothed and unprotected, who was enjoying my hospitality. I pray you will not take me for an out-and-out villain, for surely, you must admit that her story is difficult to take all that seriously at first hearing. Now I understand that *I* committed a gross error in allowing my desire to override the canons of proper behavior. I apologize to the lady, my lord. I apologize to you, my lord. And I pray you will give my apologies to her fiancé, Mr. Grantford, my lord. If you demand further satisfaction of me, I can be reached at Linscombe Park in Buckingham. My card, my lord."

Lord Dalby bowed stiffly to him and gave him his card.

Lord Leighton turned to the twins, bowed again. "My duty to you, ladies."

Sophie was shaking her head and reached out a hand to him, but he had turned on his heel and was striding toward the door. He did not stop but tore it open and walked out. They heard him go to the stairs and cry out as he descended: "Landlord, fetch my score and my horse!"

Lord Dalby stood staring at the open door for a moment. Thoughtfully, he went over to it and shut it. As he did so, he said: "Can't quite figure the fellow out. Underneath it all, he seemed a rather likable chap."

Sophie started to cry and held out her arms blindly to her sister. Sarah came to her and took her in her arms, patting her shoulder: "Sophie, love, it is quite all right. His lordship saw how it was and did the right thing. You are betrothed to Oliver and are a little upset with him at the moment. I am sure it will pass. Alan says that he is at Woodhouse. For all you know, he may have already spoken to his father and all is well. I am sure he will come with Pennie, and you know Pennie will be down upon us as soon as she has heard. Come, let us explain things to Alan before he loses patience with us."

"Oh, Sarah, I do not know! I just do not knowoo-ooh!"

Lord Dalby was frowning deeply. "I say, I am beginning to feel like a villain. This Leighton chap went out of here with an air of great sacrifice. Do you really know the fellow? *Is* he an earl?"

"Yes, Alan," said Sarah. "We had a misfortune on the road—"

"Oh, the devil you say! Were you hurt?"

"No, no, it was nothing serious. It was some trouble with one of the wheels on the chaise, but we had to park at the side of the road while the post boy went for assistance. Well, to make a long story short, Lord Leighton happened to be passing, and invited us to meet his mother and take advantage of his residence until the chaise could be restored to running order. The countess was a darling, and his lordship was most cordial. I fear he was a bit more cordial to Sophie than circumstances warranted. In any case, he came after us when we started off again, and escorted us to this inn. He had intended to see us safely to Beaumanor, you see. Now that was kind of him, don't you think?"

"Is that all there was to it? Are you making me out to be a fool? What was he doing out in the hall with Sophie as I came up?"

Sophie exploded: "Oh, blast you, Alan, I was just about to find out when you so boorishly interrupted! I could have explained if you had but given me a chance."

His lordship blinked. "I am beginning to feel a fool! I suppose next you will be telling me I owe his lordship an apology."

"You most certainly do! He is every inch a true gentleman," retorted Sophie.

"Well, I am sure it is one of those things that could not be helped, Sophie," said Sarah. "If I understand it correctly, Alan came upon you holding conversation with a perfect stranger—"

"Conversation all my eye!" exclaimed Lord

Dalby. "They were practically in each other's arms!"

"Oh, Sophie! How could you behave so poorly?!" cried Sarah.

"Truly, sister dear, it was not all that difficult!"

"Well, I must say that is a most exceptional thing for you to say, Sophie," declared Lord Dalby, "with your fiancé eating his heart out with worry over you."

"Well, he should have been with me if he loves me so much!"

Lord Dalby held up his hand. "Er—look you, have it out with him not with me. Have you eaten?"

"Yes, we dined with Lord Leighton," said Sarah. "Alan, as his lordship took all our expenses upon himself from Linslade on, I think that you not only owe him an apology but some money as well."

"Very well, it certainly begins to appear that I sadly misjudged his lordship. I shall send him a note and a sum once I have returned to London."

"Why do you not call upon him, my lord?" suggested Sophie.

"I am sure it will be less embarrassing for all concerned if I restrict myself to the mails. Well, now I had best send Jepperson down for his supper and, come to think of it, I myself have got me a hole in my midriff to drive a coach-and-six through. We shall talk some more, my ladies, as soon as your sister arrives, as I expect that she will shortly, the darling."

Sarah pleaded: "May we sit with you, Alan?

They have got a little dining room where we dined with Lord Leighton."

"Of course. You may order a sweet while I dig into something a deal more substantial. Come along, then."

Chapter 15

While he ate, Lord Dalby pieced together as best he could all that had occurred since the twins had departed London, and made loud complaint to Sarah that, if she did not settle Percy down and into his new position as clerk to his lordship, he'd begin to look about for someone else.

"Oh, but you could never do such a thing to me, Alan. You know you could not. Truly, it will be but a little while longer before Sophie and Oliver settle their affairs, and then all will be peaceful again, just as it was before. I swear it."

His lordship laughed. "Some peace, indeed! But it would be an improvement over this kiting about the country, I will admit." He lifted his bumper of ale and went on: "Here's to what goes for peace and comfort with the Sandringham ladies!"

He took a deep drink and set the glass down just as the door opened to allow Lady Dalby to come bursting in. Right behind her was Percy, no one else.

For a moment, she paused at the threshold and stared at the twins. Lord Dalby, grinning a welcome at her, rose from his chair and held out his arms. She rushed into them, and they embraced in the sight of all.

Sarah and Sophie, gleefully leaped from their seats and came to the happily reunited couple and clamored to be heard; but his lordship and his lady, after an interminable separation of almost two whole days, were completely lost to the world for some minutes.

Percy, distinctly annoyed, for he had a score to settle with her, pulled Sarah away and said: "You stole my money!"

For answer, Sarah chortled and threw her arms about his neck, hugging him close. "Oh, Percy, I missed you so!" she cried and planted a loving kiss upon his lips. It quite took his breath away, rendering him incapable of developing his case against her. Under the spell of his love once more, the warmth of her welcome, to say nothing of the enthusiasm she was now demonstrating, was worth something more than a few wallets filled with notes.

For the moment, Sophie felt dreadfully out of things. She went to the door of the dining room and peered out into the taproom. Still, there was no sign of Oliver. Perhaps he is engaged in seeing to the carriage, she thought—but surely, he could have left it for the hostlers to worry about in his rush to greet her. She turned and her eyes were filled with envy as she regarded first her older sister in the arms of her husband and then her twin in the arms of her fiancé. It was more than she could bear, and her eyes filled with tears. Where was Oliver at a time like this? She was sure that she had never needed him more than at this very instant—and he was not here!

She went over to Lady Dalby and tugged at her sleeve. "Pennie, Pennie! Why is Oliver not with you?" she demanded.

Lady Dalby planted one more kiss upon her husband's lips and pushed him away, a little breathlessly. "Now, Alan, that is enough for the time being. I have got to see to these very badly behaved young lady sisters of mine."

"Pennie, Alan said that Oliver was with you! Why has he not come?"

"Before I respond to your inquiry, my pet—Sarah, this concerns you as well! Percy! Leave her alone, do you hear. I have a few words to say to my sisters. This escapade must not go unrewarded—"

"Oh, Pennie, we know all that and, of course, we are deeply sorry for any trouble we may have put you to," said Sarah, coming over to her and taking Sophie's hand.

"Well then, if you know all that, why did you do it in the first place? And to steal Percy's money—it is incredible that two sisters of mine could have fallen so low!"

Sophie turned to Percy and said: "As for the money, Percy, you may rest easy on that score, for it was I who stole it from you, not Sarah. In any case, it was your fault."

"M-my fault!" stammered Percy, turning a look of appeal on Sarah.

She nodded and said: "Indeed, it was, love. You did say that there was enough money in your keeping to pay the fare home for Oliver and yourself, did you not?"

"I may have, but I do not see that it was of any consequence," he replied with a frown.

"Well, it most certainly was of consequence—to Sophie, for that was where she wished to travel to. As you had the correct amount, it was only natural that she should avail herself of it."

"I do not see that that is natural at all!" he protested.

"Well, what if I had taken it?"

"I thought you had and I had prepared a few choice words for you—er—but I seem to have been sidetracked," he said with a grin.

"Well, it has always been share and share alike with Sophie and me. You know that very well. Now, as you are mine—or as good as—your money is mine, and since all that I have I share with Sophie, what could be more natural than her borrowing *my* money?"

"That is purely nonsense! Why, the very idea! The next thing you know you will be sharing—

what I mean to say, it was all right when you were sisters—that is, I mean to say you are sisters and always will be, of course—er, the thing is you can carry this sharing bit too far, by damn, and I shall not stand for it! It has got to be altogether different when you are married, don't you see?"

"All right, my sweet, I shall not carry it so far. I shall be quite content to share all you have got with just me."

"That's better," he said, very satisfied. Then a thought struck him, and he looked helplessly at Lord Dalby, who was laughing. "I do believe my love has just done me up proper, my lord," he said plaintively.

"You are quite right, Percy, old thing, and let it be a lesson to you. 'Tis a perilous thing to wed a Sandringham. They are filled with the notion that they own a chap."

"Are you complaining, my lord?" asked Lady Dalby, in a sweet tone.

"No, my lady, for there is a small compensation or two that makes the business more than a little worthwhile—which tends to convince me that our friend, Oliver, is carrying things beyond foolishness if he had not the wit to accompany you this evening."

"Yes, what about Oliver? Why is he not here?" demanded Sophie.

Lady Dalby sighed and shook her head. "I am puzzled by the lad's behavior this day. Perhaps Percy has some idea."

Everyone turned to look at Percy as, one by one,

they found themselves chairs beside the table and sat down. He remained standing and donned a thoughtful expression, thrusting his hand between the buttons of his waistcoat.

"It is awfully hard to say what is going on with friend Oliver at the moment." He turned his gaze on Sophie and shook his head. "My dear Sophie, I have not had all that much time to speak with my friend, but the little that he has told me does not bode well for the business. It seems that he is engaged in talks with his father and—"

"Well, heavens, that is all I could have asked!" exclaimed Sophie, her face brightening into a relieved smile. "If our having gone off has moved Oliver to face his father on his own, then I say things are going swimmingly indeed!"

"Well, I hope you are right, dear sister—you don't mind if I call you that, do you? You will be sister to me soon," said Percy.

Sophie smiled and nodded.

"The trouble with Oliver is that he himself is having some doubts— Now, I pray you will not misunderstand me. These doubts do not originate with him but with his father. I know this to be a fact because Oliver has always been true to his love for you even as I have been to the love I bear for my Sarah. It is just that Mr. Grantford is a most forceful individual, and when he is intent upon getting his own way, he is more than one can withstand—at least Oliver is having trouble in that quarter, I do believe."

Sophie was biting her lip, and her brow was

wrinkled with doubt. "Perhaps if I went over to speak with Mr. Grantford, it would help. At least then we would know what his objection to me was, if any. I do not think it is something Oliver would care to repeat to me."

Lady Dalby shook her head. "Nothing doing, young lady! This entire idea of yours was a most unsuitable thing! A lady does not go to plead with the father of her betrothed for acceptance. That is for her fiancé to do—and it is for her fiancé to make up his mind as between his father's wishes and his bride-to-be's."

"My sweet, I believe you have left out one party's wishes in the matter," said Lord Dalby, "and they must be the most telling of the lot. What of Oliver's wishes in the matter? Until the lad knows his own mind, until he knows precisely what he wants—and I have my doubts that he ever did—there is nothing more to be said on our side of it. Sophie, I am sure you have got to agree with me on that score. For Oliver to set any store on his father's objections, no matter what they may be, speaks poorly of his devotion to you and puts into question his own suitability for the match."

"But we are betrothed," she pointed out in a reasoned manner, without any emotion.

Said Lady Dalby: "Be that as it may, but the entire point of an engagement, I believe, is to give the couple a chance to think about it—although I will admit that our honorable gentlemen of the courts" —and she gave her husband a pointed look— "think of it as a contract signed, sealed and irrevocable. I cannot believe it was ever intended so. A marriage, yes; but an engagement?—I say no!"

"My dearly beloved countess, I admire your knowledge of the law, but you must remember that these rules were laid down by far wiser minds than ours—"

"Nonsense, my lord. Far older, yes; but who is to say far wiser? In any case, they were all of them males, and what do they know about anything?"

"That argument will never hold water in court, but then, as you point out, all of us judges are indeed males. In any event, my sweet, be at peace. I know I can never carry the day with you within the four walls of our home and so I must bow to your illogical logic—"

"Well, I think that we are foolish to go on sitting in this uncomfortable inn when we have a beautiful home to go to not more than a half hour's ride away, my lord. I suggest that we are all a bit tired from being so overwrought for so long. It is late and we need our rest. We shall have all of tomorrow to talk about this. There is no rush."

"Er—my pet," said Lord Dalby, "I hesitate to mention it, but I fear that, although the wheels of justice will not come to a complete halt in my absence, they may well be slowed some. I do not think it will make my brother justices too happy to have to handle my cases for very long. I pray, therefore, that we can get all this business resolved so that I can get back to my court without too much delay."

"In that case, Alan, you shall have to pay a call upon Mr. Grantford and son and learn how the wind stands in that quarter."

"Yes, I feared you would say something like that. I could almost wish that Sophie had managed the bit on her own. It would have saved me the trouble. Oh, well, so be it. I shall look up the gentlemen in the morning."

Chapter 16

It was past one in the afternoon, and Sarah and Lady Dalby were seated on a pair of high straight-backed Elizabethan chairs in the great reception hall of Beaumanor. They were both of them occupied with embroidering some cushion covers that they had discovered in a cupboard that must not have been opened in over fifty years. The materials had been wrapped carefully by some ancient Desford dame of another age and were quite well preserved. It was not much, certainly the design was nothing that Lady Dalby cared to use; but the work was something to keep them occupied while they awaited Lord Dalby's return from the Grantfords'.

Sophie was not working at anything. Her share

of the materials lay neglected upon another chair, while she walked slowly back and forth the length of the great hall, stopping every now and again at the tall windows to part the curtains and peer outside.

Finally she exclaimed: "Oh, I do wish he would hurry back! He has been away for so long! Oh, I tell you it should have been I who went to call upon them! It would never have taken me so long as this! After all, it is quite a simple matter. Either Oliver loves me or he does not. What is there about it to call for protracted discussion?"

"Sophie, do sit down before you wear yourself out," admonished Lady Dalby. "You just do not understand these things, child. It is not merely a question of Oliver's devotion to you. There are other matters that have to be considered. There is the question of the marriage settlements: How much will Mr. Grantford settle upon Oliver? Remember how important that must be to Oliver and you, for he has no means of support at the moment—and then there is the question of how much you are to bring to the marriage. If you are to be secure in your independence, then funds or other items of value, such as land or shares, must be settled upon you—"

"It was never so complicated with Alan and you, Pennie! I do not recall any great haggling going on before you and he stood up together."

"Well, it was different with us, don't you see? Alan has more than he can possibly need, so that he could look where it pleased him for a bride. He could as easily support a judge's daughter as a duke's daughter. I was just so fortunate to be the former, which, queer chap, he seems to have preferred."

"All right. But what of Percy and Sarah? There has not been a word as to settlements with them. Sarah cannot bring to her marriage a penny more than I can—and a penny is about all it can be—"

"Dearest, do not fret yourself. Sarah's turn will come. I am sure that Viscount Deverill has yet to be heard from upon that score—or has Percy had anything to say to you about it, Sarah?"

Sarah shook her head. "No, Pennie, not a thing. Do you think I have cause to worry?"

"Not really, for Percy has his independence, and the stipend he receives from Alan as his clerk will not be mere shillings. In your case the viscount's approval is sought merely as a matter of courtesy, don't you see. Unfortunately, it is not the case with Oliver, since his father controls the purse strings. Truly, it is a shame that Oliver had not associated himself with his father in the business way so that, by this time, he might have amassed something to support a bride on."

A horse drew up outside, and Sophie made a mad dash for the door. She swung it open, looked out and turned back, her face filled with a look of disappointment.

"It is only Percy," she said, unhappily.

"Only Percy!" cried Sarah, dropping her work and running to the door.

Percy came through at just the right moment to

catch his love in his arms and plant a kiss on her lips. Then, looking into her face with a great smile, he declared: "The viscount has come through in great form, by Jupiter! He is settling a third of the Deverill holdings on me! Now what do you say to that, my darling?!"

His darling suitably rewarded the father with a passionate salute to the son, while Lady Dalby arose to congratulate the fortunate couple.

Sophie came and kissed her sister and then went to stand by the door, her face quite a study. There was a touch of frustration in it, and there was a touch of anger in it, but most of all, there was impatience in it. She stayed there looking out, while Lady Dalby, Sarah and Percy chatted excitedly about the good news.

She was completely absorbed in her own thoughts, lost to her surroundings, so that it was Lady Dalby who first heard the carriage coming up the drive.

"That must be my lord!" she cried, leaping up from her chair. She went over to Sophie and took her by the hands, waiting with her for Lord Dalby's appearance. Sarah and Percy, holding hands, came and joined them.

The carriage drew up, and his lordship descended out of it in a deliberate fashion. His face was unsmiling, even as he waved at the little group that was awaiting him with breathless anticipation. He came up the few stairs to the threshold and, looking at his wife, slowly shook his head.

"Oh, no, Alan! Not bad news!" she cried.

He said as he came inside: "I fear it is so! Never have I felt so bedeviled, so utterly at a loss to work things out. Dearest Sophie, I did my level best in your cause, but I was defeated on all counts. My dear, the thing that is the hardest to bear is that I am forced to admit that Oliver is truly a branch of the tree that bore him. He was absolutely no help at all. If anything, I had to contend with him as much as I had to contend with Mr. Grantford himself. It was a losing battle all the way."

Sophie merely stared glumly at him for a moment. Then she took a breath and said: "It is over, is it not?"

"Yes, my dear, I am afraid it is. Actually, now that I have been through the wars with the Grantfords, I am sort of relieved. I am deeply sorry for the disappointment and the pain that this news must occasion for you, but I am relieved. It has shown me the Grantfords in their true light. Up to this time, I had taken their measure from the little acquaintance I had with Oliver and your particular estimates of the chap—and, too, as he was Percy's bosom beau, that counted heavily with me in his favor. But, now, I have been granted a sight and a hearing of Grantford and son and I am relieved that I shall not have to count them amongst my in-laws, ever. I pray this opinion of mine does not cause you greater pain."

"Thank you, Alan, for all you have done in my behalf—but I do not know that it is such a disappointment after all," said Sophie, quite calmly. "Perhaps, it is because I had begun to lose my faith in Oliver. I—I think I came away from London more to save my good opinion of him than for any other reason. Truly, it is not right that a lady speak to her fiancé's father for such a purpose. I am beginning to feel quite foolish about the business now."

"Then you will agree to release Oliver from his pledge?"

"Of course. I bear him no ill will—but I am curious to know his reasons. Was it something I had done?"

"No, nothing like that at all. It was Mr. Grantford's intransigence that swayed Oliver. In a way, one might have thought that Oliver was just being noble about the business. As Mr. Grantford was adamant about cutting Oliver off without a cent, so long as Oliver could not support a wife, he must renounce his heartfelt wishes in the matter. Understanding that this might be the sticking place, I offered to make a handsome settlement on both of you—truly not as much as might have come to Oliver from his father but enough to see you both comfortable. A look from his father and Oliver rejected it. As I gathered from a confusion of reasons and, in my opinion, witless convictions, Oliver is to marry blood and at his father's direction. It makes no sense to me at all."

"Oh, the poor lad!" exclaimed Lady Dalby, filled with sympathy.

"Oh, do not waste your pity on the fellow. He had his chance to choose and, in the final analysis proved himself a true son of his father—a snob, the son of a snob."

Percy shook his head. "It is sad. For all of our lives, Oliver and I thought alike—until now. It is as though I have lost me a dear friend."

Lord Dalby turned to Sophie. "My dear, I know how weak this may sound to you, but if there is anything I can do for you in this unhappy time, you know I shall do my best to please you."

"Thank you, Alan. Now, if you will excuse me, I should like to be alone."

She took a few steps away and then stopped and looked to Sarah. Sarah immediately turned to Percy. He smiled slightly, took her hand in his and gave it a little squeeze as he nodded. Sarah kissed him and turned away to join her sister. They went out of the great hall hand in hand.

Lady Dalby murmured: "It is so sad. Now, Sarah will wed and Sophie will only be her bridesmaid. Oh, I wish it would not be so!"

The next morning breakfast at Beaumanor promised to be a sumptuous affair. The staff had been without a sight of their lord and lady for four months and were out to do themselves proud. More than a few of the servants had ambitions to be promoted to the Desford London establishment, and all of them held their lady in great affection and respect, having had her for neighbor at Bellflower Cottage these many years.

It was past eight o'clock in the morning, and the meal was being served at table instead of buffet.

Lord and Lady Dalby and Miss Sarah Sandringham were down for breakfast, and all would have been well except for the fact that they had waited fifteen minutes for Miss Sophie to make her appearance before beginning to dine. A maid had been sent up to inquire of her indisposition, and they were now awaiting word.

"Sarah, is there something that you are not telling us?" inquired Lady Dalby.

Sarah shook her head and went on eating.

"Well, was she coming down to breakfast when you left her?"

Sarah replied: "Yes, Pennie. In fact, I thought that she would be right behind me. She merely said that she had to return to our room for something. I cannot imagine what is detaining her."

At that moment the maid returned to inform her ladyship that Miss Sandringham was taken by a sudden indisposition and would not be down.

"Did you discover her in bed?"

"No, your ladyship. Miss Sandringham was seated by the window and appeared quite well."

"Then I do not understand. Did she at least give some indication of the nature of this sudden indisposition?"

"No, your ladyship. Shall I inquire?"

"No. That will be all, Madge." She turned to Lord Dalby and said: "My lord, I pray you will excuse me, but I must look in on Sophie. I feel quite uneasy about this sudden indisposition of hers. We may have to call in the doctor."

Lord Dalby was looking concerned. "Of course, love. Do whatever you think is best."

Her ladyship left the table and went up to the twins' chamber. She knocked and entered without waiting for a response.

"Sophie, what is wrong, child?"

"Oh, it is nothing, Pennie. I just do not feel up to having breakfast. I pray you will not let it disturb you."

"Well, I am disturbed. It is so unlike you to come down with some complaint and Sarah not affected likewise. Do you hurt anywhere?"

"No, no, Pennie, I assure you it is nothing. I am just not hungry at the moment. I mean to say we all of us suffer a loss of appetite every now and again, do we not?"

"I dare say—but I have the feeling that this is not anything like that. Sarah has no complaint and is quite busy with her food at the moment—"

"Well, what has she to complain about?" Sophie snapped, her voice quite bitter.

"Ah, I suspect that we are coming to it now. Sophie, something is bothering you. I know it and I know further, from your tone, it is no physical complaint. You are terribly disappointed in Oliver, are you not? It is a blow to know that the man you love does not love you in truth. Come, Sophie, I am your sister and I love you dearly. Let me help you. Tell me exactly what you are feeling."

"Oh, Pennie, it is not Oliver! I could not care less about Oliver. He was a disappointment from the beginning. It—it is s-something else."

"Well, I am relieved to hear that it is not Oliver that has set you down so badly—although it must have come as the greatest shock—but if it is not your disappointment in Oliver, then what can it be if it is not a physical complaint? One's appetite does not disappear for no reason at all."

"I am sure it is a passing thing. Why do you not go down and finish your breakfast, Pennie? I would just as soon be by myself for a bit anyway."

Lady Dalby arose and started for the door. As she raised her hand to the latch she paused, turned about and came back to Sophie. Drawing up her chair closer, she sat down and looked into her sister's face. Then she reached out her hand and placed it on Sophie's brow. At her touch, Sophie began to weep, silently, sitting stiffly with her hands clenched tightly. It lasted but a moment before she turned and threw herself into her ladyship's arms, sobbing.

Lady Dalby hugged Sophie to her until the sobs began to subside. She gave her a little shake and said, in a light but forceful tone: "Now, come, Sophie, you are acting quite missish, and that is not at all like a Sandringham female. You are acting as though your heart were broken, yet you claim that it is not Oliver. Then who can it be? Lord Fallon? He is the only gentleman in your acquaintance to whom you showed any favor at all other than Oliver."

Sophie shook her head as she dried her cheeks: "Oh, Pennie, you are so wise. There is another, but you do not know him. I—I think he likes me and I know that I like him."

Lady Dalby regarded Sophie with an air of great puzzlement. "Who is he? When can you have possibly met him and I not know about it? Oh, Sophie, have you been carrying on behind my back?"

"No, Pennie, I swear it. It came about in the most innocent way. I have already told Alan, and he met his lordship. They—they had words. Y-you see, Alan misunderstood what he saw—and then it was all too late. John left and I—I sh-shall n-never s-see him again!" she ended in a wail and the tears started to flow again.

"Alan knew about this and he never said a word to me?" exclaimed Lady Dalby, highly indignant. "Well, really! But, in heaven's name, child, what did he see that he should have been so angered?"

"I tell you it was not anything at all. John and I were in the corridor speaking when Alan came by—"

"Where? What hall?"

"At the Stag and Pheasant."

"Do you tell me that you were holding conversation with a strange man in so public a place as the corridor of an inn? I do not blame Alan for his anger. Nor can I say anything that is nice about a gentleman who would take such advantage of a young lady!"

"Oh, you are just like Alan! You will not listen! I tell you that Lord Leighton is a most unexceptional gentleman. He would have to be, to be the son of so fine and charming a lady as the countess of Leighton!"

Lady Dalby was wondering which of them was suddenly out of their depth as she stared at her sister. "Great heavens, Sophie, what do you know of any Countess Leighton?"

"I am trying to tell you. Lord Leighton took us into his home—it is called Linscombe Park—and we were introduced to the countess, his mother, and made to feel at home while our chaise was being fixed. It is a most beautiful place, not so large as Beaumanor, but kept up in a most exquisite fashion. He raises horses."

"Oh, dear, I am dreadfully confused. Pray just how old is this Lord Leighton?"

"Oh, he is older than I am, but he is never so old as Alan."

"Well, really, you make Alan sound a venerable ancient. Alan is not quite so old as *that!*"

For the first time, Sophie smiled. "Oh, you know what I mean."

Lady Dalby smiled, too. "Then you spent some time with Lord Leighton and his mother. Is that why you were so delayed in getting to Woodhouse?"

"Yes, it took forever and a day to repair the chaise that we had hired, and so the countess made us stay overnight until it was done—and then, we had only gotten a little on our way, when the earl came up with us and asked if he be allowed to join us. He felt it was a reflection on his hospitality to allow ladies to go from under his roof upon such a

journey unescorted—but I think it was because he
wished to be with me."

Lady Dalby shook her head and said: "The confusion grows. What in the world in all of this did
Alan take exception to?"

"Well, after it was too late, he did admit to have
acted the fool—but the damage was done. I am
sure that Lord Leighton has had his fill of the San-
dringhams and the Desfords."

"And this, then, is the reason that you must sit
up in your room and pine away the breakfast hour?
You have taken a liking to Lord Leighton?"

"Oh, Pennie, more than a liking! I was so
frightened that Oliver might succeed with his father
and I was so relieved that he did not. I am sure you
would love his lordship. He is such a—gentleman!
Even Alan had to admit that, but for the misunder-
standing, he was sure that he could have liked him.
I know Sarah likes him—and the countess, too! She
is such a dear lady."

Lady Dalby was now knitting her brows. She
looked up at Sophie. "What I do not still understand is, if Lord Leighton is such a fine gentleman,
why must he insist upon speaking with you in so
public a place?"

"I—do believe it was because of the kiss—"

"The kiss?! Good heavens! He kissed you in the
corridor of an inn like any common tavern wench?"

"Oh, Pennie, how can you say such a thing?!
Now you insult his lordship and your sister as well!
It was under an oak tree on his estate."

"Well, I must say he made a most trustworthy

host! Taking advantage of a young guest like that—and what were you doing with him out on his estate all by yourselves? You know better than that!"

"Of course, I do. Sarah was along with us. She just happened to turn her back for a moment."

"How very convenient," remarked Lady Dalby, her voice dripping with sarcasm.

"*I* thought so," Sophie grinned saucily.

Lady Dalby had to laugh. But she raised a hand to her brow and shook her head. "And what was the business in the inn, then?"

"I think he wished to apologize for the kiss. You see, after that we never had a chance to be alone, not in the chaise with Sarah right there, or anywhere. It was the first time in my life that I found Sarah's presence something less than desirable—but I warn you, had Alan not interfered at the worst moment, I think his lordship might well have kissed me a second time—and oh, Pennie, I am sure that I wanted it as much as he did!"

Lady Dalby sighed. "I see. Well, I dare say we shall have to do something about this or you will be claiming I did it out of jealousy that I might be the only Sandringham countess, wouldn't you?"

"Oh, but definitely, sister dear."

They smiled at each other, and Sophie threw her arms about Lady Dalby, asking: "But what can we do about it now?"

"I am not so sure, dear heart, that I have an answer, but this much I do know. As it was Alan who put his oar into it when it was not wanted, it will have to be Alan who must come up with a scheme to make things right."

"Yes. I am sure Alan can do it. He is so clever!"

They drew back from each other, and Lady Dalby said: "Now you must give me a little time to go to work with my lord. He is bound to be a bit balky at first. And then there is Lord Leighton. I mean to say you cannot be sure that his treatment at Alan's hands did not act to quench his ardor, if that was truly what it was in the first place. It could have been but a flirtation as far as he was concerned, you know."

"Oh, I am sure it was nothing like that. I could tell," said Sophie very seriously.

"Yes, and I am sure you are quite the expert in these matters."

Sophie blushed. "Well, the least that you can do is to invite Lord Leighton to call upon us the very next time he comes to London. Perhaps the countess will then respond with an invitation to come visit her, and everything will be all right."

"Well, let me consult with Alan. I will admit that the prospect of an earl as against Oliver as brother-in-law is infinitely more appealing, especially if his lordship comes up to but half the encomiums you have paid him."

Chapter 17

The countess dowager of Leighton was sitting in her own little writing chamber reading a novel, hired out of the library in Linslade, when she heard a rider approaching the house. It was but the early afternoon of the day after John had departed to see after their lovely young guests and she frowned. She put down her book, removed her spectacles, rose and went to the window. Peering out she saw that indeed it was her son coming home. Her frown deepened, and she left the chamber to go out to greet him. As she came out the front door, he was in the act of dismounting. One look at his drawn face told her that it was more than his ride that had put the lines in it.

As he came forward to greet her, she smiled and

lifted her cheek to his kiss. Taking him by the hand, she began to lead him into the house.

"Come, John, we must talk. Things did not go well, I see."

"As ever, Mother, you are right on the mark."

They went into a small drawing room just off the reception hall and sat down, her ladyship having given orders to prepare a cold collation for his lordship's refection.

They settled themselves, and the countess said: "Considering the hour of your return, you can have barely had time to see them to their doorstep before you started for home. Were you not made welcome?"

"I have been slow in my journey back. I had not the heart to go at any pace. No, I never did see them so far as their destination. It was at an inn in Leicester that we parted company and under the most unpleasant circumstances. I had the pleasure—or should I say, mispleasure—of making the acquaintance of their brother-in-law, the earl of Dalby. Well, really, I cannot blame him for thinking what he did. I behaved like an utter idiot. You see how it was, Mother, I had the strongest desire to speak with Miss Sophie alone, and it was quite impossible to do so, for Miss Sarah was always about. I suppose that is the way with twins—but, anyway, I drew her out in the corridor just to make my apology for my misbehavior—although you may split me if I would not have kissed her again—when his lordship, just arriving, discovered us in a most compromising situation—"

"Gracious me, how compromising could it have been out in an inn corridor? Good heavens, John, what were you doing with the girl, anyway?"

"Oh, dash it all, we were just about to speak with each other, but he could not know that. After all he did not know me from Adam, and there was his young and beautiful sister-in-law in the arms of a complete stranger. It is no wonder he flew off the handle with me—and yet I could not help but like the fellow. He seemed no sort of stuffy judge to me. In any case, we went in together to the girls' room and unraveled things a bit, but even as we did so, Miss Sophie explained quite clearly—too clearly, I thought—how she had been on her way to speak with her prospective father-in-law about her forthcoming marriage to this Oliver person. After that, there was no further point to my presence in their company. I cannot imagine an elderly gentleman who could resist the appeal of that little charmer. So you see, my lady mother, I was never in the running, for all her seeming warmth to me. I must conclude that Miss Sophie is nothing more than a little flirt, and this Oliver is bound to have more than his fill with her for wife." He sighed. "Still, I would give anything to be able to trade places with him."

The countess thought a bit, and then she said: "It is too bad. Neither of the girls struck me as being that sort. Well, son, perhaps you ought to go for a repairing lease in London."

He laughed. "Yes, you put it right. Everyone comes out to the country to ease their woes and restore themselves to health, but I must to the city for my solace. Perhaps I shall—but I think that I should prefer to sit about a bit. Meeting with Miss Sophie has made me marvelously dissatisfied with my life at the moment. I shall have to do something about it, I am sure."

"Well, that will be a wonder. My thanks to Miss Sophie if she is the cause that will move you to end your single state."

She looked at him for a moment. "You do not think that there is yet a chance? Nothing is certain in this world, and if there is any chance at all, I did take to the girls and would love to have them for friends."

"It is quite hopeless, my lady. I cannot imagine that we shall ever hear of the ladies again."

She shrugged her shoulders. "Oh well, so be it, I dare say. I pray you will think about London seriously, son."

Lord Leighton did begin to think about London seriously. He had not been to the city in years, having no business to attend to there and having no particular fondness for what went for companionship there, either. He had been satisfied to devote himself to the task of building up a stable of spotless reputation, and It had taken up his time and all of his thoughts. Now, his reputation as a nonpareil breeder of excellent beasts brought him all the custom he could wish for, and the challenge was gone. Perhaps he might have gone on with it in peace if nothing had occurred to ruffle his thinking. Unfortunately, his mere offer of assistance to a pair of ladies on the road had had such consequences as to insure that he would be a long time in regaining his peace of mind. London was not the place where he could find his lost ease, for that was where *she* hailed from. He knew very well that if he traveled to London, it would be with the sole purpose of calling upon Miss Sophie—or would she be Mrs. Grantford by that time? The thought caused a pang in his breast, and he muttered an oath.

He looked out of the window and surveyed the grounds of Linscombe Park. It was a sight to give him great pride and satisfaction. It had done so every day of his life these past years but not today. Today, it was just a space filled with grounds and structures, all well tended but raising no particular emotion in his breast. All that was there was a hollowness, a pointless emptiness, and it resolved itself into one monstrous ache.

She could have filled it. With her at his side, the scene would have been filled with delightful lights and shadows, and there would be happiness in it for him, even more than pride. How strange life was! A few hours, a day, and all was changed. Contentment was transformed to dissatisfaction, peace to unrest—and he was helpless to do a thing about it. Ah, well, her ladyship was right! He could not remain at home to brood on it. He would have to leave for a time and find himself something to restore his appetite for living. As long as he was about it, he might as well begin seriously to look for a wife—but not in London.

If not London, then where? Bath? Tunbridge

Wells? Cheltenham? None of those watering places
appealed to him. Ah, what about Wales? He had
always cherished a desire to see what he could do
with Welsh stock—the tough and hardy little Welsh
pony. Perhaps he could incorporate some of its
more desirable characteristics into a line of
hunters—or think about refining the breed for
mounting young folk. It was a deal more of a horse
than the Shetland— Ah, but what of a wife? He
would never find a wife in Wales. He could not
even speak the language.

No matter. It was a change he was in need of.
After six months or so of studying the breed on its
own ranges, he would return immensely benefited
and more in a mood to seek a countess for himself.
He might even leave directions with his mother to
keep her eye out for him with regard to likely prospects. He was sure he would not have to spell
anything out for her. She was always most
understanding.

He felt a little better after coming to the decision. He now had regained some direction to his
life, and although it went very little way to restoring his peace, it did give him a bit of ease and allow him to regain his perspective.

Having made his decision and feeling much better for having done so, Lord Leighton found his interest in his avocation restored, and plunged back
into the business of horse breeding and rearing. He
was so much at ease with himself now, that the idea
of going out to Wales actually began to fade, and it

lost much of its urgency. Although he discussed it with his mother, that was all he did about it. When she asked him when he had it in mind to proceed with it, he answered that he would get on with it in good time. But, at last, the matter of getting away from his usual pursuits gained the day with him, and he came to the countess and declared he was now ready. In a week he would leave her for a bit. He was going off to London.

Her ladyship laughed in his face and told him that he was about to make a fool of himself.

"Oh, truly, my lady, I have no intention of seeking out Miss Sophie. After all, London is quite a large city, and I am sure that my daily rounds there will not take me into the vicinity of Cavendish Square."

"Is that where they live?"

"Yes, they are staying with their sister, the countess, for the season. In any case, I am sure that her wedding plans are well forward, if not already executed. There can be no danger to me even if I should happen to run into her."

"At least, you recognize that it does constitute a danger to you. Why do you not go out to Wales? Next season you can go to London when there will be no danger to speak of."

He smiled. "Oh, we are making too much of it, I assure you. I am a grown man and quite capable of maintaining good sense in my dealings. I assure you there is naught to worry about, and as Wales is the last place to find a congenial female, it makes no sense to go out there when I am in this mood. You have wanted me to get out and mix with people for the longest time, have you not? Well, London is most certainly the place for that, never Wales. Yes, it makes a deal of sense to go to London where the greatest gathering of eligible ladies is. It is no more than what you have been saying."

"Had I known that you would have fallen head over heels with a little flirt, I am sure I should have held my tongue. You know, John, the more I think of it, the more I am impressed with the fact that this Miss Sandringham could not have been very nice. She led you on even when she knew that she was already promised and engaged upon an enterprise that demonstrates how desperate was her case. I mean to say, it is unheard of for a lady to sue for the approval of prospective in-laws—"

"Yes, I know and I have had it on my mind, too. I am sure it must make for a coolness between us which, you will admit, puts an entirely different complexion on things, making of a trip to London at this time no special thing."

"Are you sure that that is how you feel about it?"

"Quite sure. You have not a thing to worry about."

"Well, I am not about to say what you ought or ought not do, son. Still, I strongly advise you to avoid their vicinity."

"It is quite all right. As I am not about to call upon them and they are not about to call upon me—I am sure not to be in Lord Dalby's good graces—the chances of our meeting are not worth mentioning."

"Now that must be the silliest thing you could have said. John, you will be going to affairs and you will be attending balls at Almack's. You are a very eligible gentleman and, once it is known that you are in town, you will be deluged with invitations. You are *bound* to run into one or the other of the girls. And, since they are as alike as two peas in a pod, either one of them is bound to remind you strongly of this recent unfortunate episode."

"Perhaps, but I am not about to hide from them or anybody else. I think it is imperative that I go to London if only to prove to myself that I am no fool and can maintain an imperturbable front before the Desfords. I would not have them think any less of me than they do already."

"If I could believe that you are saying what you mean and not disguising from yourself a wish to be near the girl, I should be much easier in my mind."

"Be easy in your mind, my lady. It is precisely as I have said."

Although he had put on a brave front before his mother, Lord Leighton suffered grave doubts as to his true intentions. As a result, the very next day he discovered he was in no greater rush to go off to London than he had been to Wales. But, as he had said it would be a week before he would start, he put the entire business out of his mind and spent the rest of the morning walking about the grounds pondering it.

He resolved to go down to the stables and see how things were progressing there after the midday meal, but as he was not hungry when noontime arrived, he continued his perambulations, trying to come to some conclusions so that he could get on with whatever he ought to be doing.

He was out upon the great lawn before the house when his musings were interrupted by a fine curricle coming up the drive. It was adorned with the dust of travel and a device, unknown to him, but signaling that the proprietor of the vehicle was on a rank with himself, an earl. He frowned as he started for it, while the curricle was brought to a stop and two gentlemen dismounted.

He immediately recognized Lord Dalby, and his heart sank within him as he guessed whom the younger gentleman undoubtedly was. He was extremely relieved to have the opportunity of meeting with the gentlemen out upon the lawn away from the sight and hearing of the countess. This was bound to be a most embarrassing encounter for him.

His face a mask for his emotions, he walked to meet the gentlemen coming toward him. He did not hold out his hand, but he came to a stop and said: "Dalby, I was sure that we said all that there was to say back at the Stag and Pheasant—but I see we have not. I take it that the gentleman accompanying you is Mr. Grantford come to seek an apology for my behavior to his fiancée. If it will satisfy you and permit a quick termination to this unpleasant meeting, I do hereby make my apology to you, Mr. Grantford."

Percy was blinking in confusion and flushing with embarrassment as Lord Dalby shook his head vehemently and held out his hand. "No, no, my lord, you have got the wrong end of the stick! Quite! It is the other way around. I am come to make my apology to you for having flown off the handle with you before I ever became acquainted with the facts of the case. I regret deeply to have to admit that I was something lacking in judicial detachment at the time. It is particularly distressing in light of the fact, as my sisters-in-law informed me, that I am in your debt for the protection and the hospitality you afforded them. I pray you will forgive my excessive concern for a pair of lovely scatterbrains and give me your hand on it."

Lord Leighton accepted Lord Dalby's hand with no great enthusiasm and nodded.

Lord Dalby shook it and went on: "I would take it as a great favor if I could pay my respects to Lady Leighton. The ladies were full of praise for your lady mother, and I should be remiss if I did not thank her for her condescension to my relations."

Percy cleared his throat, and Lord Dalby turned to him with a questioning look.

Percy placed a finger on his chest and nodded to Lord Leighton.

"Oh, yes! Ah, Leighton, you must see how very confused I am to have omitted presenting my companion to you. I have the privilege of making known to you the honorable Percival Deverill who has graciously agreed to serve as clerk to me in my judicial capacity—and is Sarah's intended."

Lord Leighton reached out and shook hands with Percy. "My dear fellow, I am delighted. Indeed I am," he said with a deal more enthusiasm than he had shown to Lord Dalby.

Percy grinned and said: "My lord, I am forever grateful for your kindness to my fiancée and her sister."

"They are both of them charming ladies. I need no thanks, Deverill."

Then his lordship turned to Lord Dalby. "It is not that I am a glutton for gratitude, Dalby, but it does appear to me that there is someone missing."

Lord Dalby's face fell. "Indeed, I know what you mean, Leighton. There should have been another young gentleman with me, but he has asked for his pledge back, and it was given him. It grieves me to have to tell you that Miss Sophie remains unattached."

"Oh, how very sad," remarked Lord Leighton, having to bite his lips to hold back the shout of high glee that threatened to explode within him. "Well, I am more than happy to have had you gentlemen call upon me and I should deem it a privilege to have you come meet with my mother, the countess. She would be heartbroken and highly wroth with me if I neglected to bring you to her.

Come, it is a short but pleasant stroll back to the house. I shall send for your rig to be brought up Now, I do hope that you will stay the night with us. It is too late to return. . . ."

Chapter 18

They were gathered in the countess's favorite sitting room, seated about her in a circle of chairs, and the conversation was in full flow.

". . . And you will be staying the night, Lord Dalby, will you not?"

"Alas, my lady, it is not possible. We are due in London—in fact, I am overdue in my colleagues' estimation, I am sure. I have had to leave the bench because of my wife's sisters' escapade. I dropped by here to make especially sure that Lord Leighton understood my feelings with regard to him. It was a most unfortunate set of circumstances, as you must understand, and the matter begged for rectification."

"I see. So this is Miss Sarah's gentleman, is it?

Mr. Deverill, you must know how fortunate you are to have won for yourself such a dear and charming young lady."

"Indeed, my lady, it is not something I have to be reminded of. I have always been devoted to Sarah and I count myself fortunate for having grown up alongside of her."

Her ladyship frowned. "It is too bad the other young man could not be present. I should have dearly loved to have seen Miss Sophie's choice."

"My lady," said Lord Leighton, with a glint in his eye and a slight smile on his lips, "Lord Dalby has informed me that Miss Sophie's troth has been revoked. She has no gentleman at the moment."

"How very fort—er—I mean to say, the poor, poor dear. I dare say the young lady is quite over-come. She was so devoted to what's-his-name that she was quite determined to ask for his hand from his father."

"Er—well, I would not say that Miss Sophie is all that discommoded by the event," said Lord Dalby.

"If anything, I should say that Sophie was some-thing relieved," added Percy. "Of all of us, I ven-ture to say that it is only I who am disappointed. You see, Oliver is my friend from childhood, and it seemed so apt that he and I should each of us wed a twin—but, then, things never do work out *all* around, do they?"

"And where are the young ladies now, my lord?" inquired the countess. "It would have been so nice if you could have brought them along with you."

"They are awaiting us in the company of their sister, my wife. I suppose I ought to admit that they all pressed me unmercifully to do my duty to Lord Leighton. I had to admit to the justice of their demands and so I have come—but, as it could have been possibly an embarrassing encounter, it was thought wisest to have the ladies remain in Linslade while I paid this call. I am so relieved that all has turned out so well and now am disappointed that they did not accompany me. I hope that when you come to London you will do us the honor of calling upon us, Lady Leighton."

"Indeed, but I shall not fail. In fact, my son intends going in that direction shortly. I have no doubt that you will be seeing something of him during his sojourn in the city."

"My lord, you may count on it," seconded Lord Leighton with a grin.

Lord Dalby then rose up, and Percy did the same. Bowing to her ladyship, he declared: "It has been a great pleasure, my lady, meeting with you and your son. I shall be looking forward to a renewal of our acquaintance in the near future. Now we must run. I do not wish to keep my ladies waiting—"

There was some sort of bustling out in the corridor, and a footman came bursting into the room, gasping: "Her ladyship, the right honorable countess of—"

"Alan, they are gone! They have disappeared from the inn!" cried Lady Dalby, rushing over to her husband in a most distraught manner.

"For God's sake, Pennie, where are your manners?!" he exclaimed, highly annoyed.

Lady Dalby stopped, a look of embarrassment crimsoning her cheeks. "Oh, I beg your pardon, Countess," she said, making a curtsy.

Lord Dalby took her by the arm and led her up to the dowager. "My lady, this poor excuse for a wife is Lady Dalby. As you have heard, we must leave you now in a bit of a rush. Those infernal sisters-in-law of mine are up to their old tricks again. Pennie, are you quite sure that they have gone off again?"

"I am quite positive. They claimed to be overtired, and Sophie was looking particularly peaked, so I hired them a room for their repose until your return. Need I say more? They slipped quietly away. Oh, I shall not be responsible for what I shall do to them when we get them back again!"

Lord Leighton came to Lady Dalby and said: "My dear countess, there is no time for formalities, but I am John Linscombe, Lord Leighton. Now you say—"

But Lady Dalby was looking at him, her eyebrows raised on high, obvious approval in her face. "So *you* are Lord Leighton!" She turned and looked to Lord Dalby, a quizzical smile on her face. "I think I am beginning to understand a few things, my lord."

He laughed and threw out his hands in a gesture of helplessness. "*Yes!* But what is there to be done about it?"

Lord Leighton said, impatiently but in good humor: "I know what is to be done about it. My lord? My lady, by your leave?"

"You have some idea of where they have gone?" asked Lady Dalby.

He clenched one fist and nodded. "It *has* to be there!"

"Yes," said Lady Leighton. "I quite agree, John. Do you go and fetch them to us—and, son, there is no great rush. These lovely people are staying with us for a bit. I shall insist upon it. Now, shoo!"

Lord Leighton was chuckling as he strode from the room.

Once outside the house, he headed directly for the stables, calling for a horse to be readied. One was provided in quick time, and he mounted and rode off.

He came to the oak grove by the stream and dismounted. Yes, they were here. There were two horses standing in a nearby field. He started for the shady oak that was now become so special to him. He was some few strides from it and could see there was someone sitting under it when a voice to his left called out: "It is overlong, my lord, that you have kept us waiting."

He turned, a great smile on his lips; but the smile faded rapidly as he saw it was Sarah stepping forth from behind a tall shrub.

He bowed to her. "My dear Sarah, I am sure I shall love you like a sister, but at the moment, like so many before, your company is more than I care for."

She laughed. "I was just leaving, my lord. How

fortunate for me that you came along. You can escort me back to the house."

He-chuckled. "Blast you, you know the way! Now hop to it, my dear, or you shall rue every minute you delay."

"Well, I am sure I can take a hint no matter how broad it is. Good day to you, my lord."

"Come, the least I can do is to assist you to mount."

"No, thank you, my lord. I can manage quite well by myself and would not detain you lest you carry out your awful threat."

She slipped away toward the horses. As he proceeded onward, he heard her ride off.

Sophie smiled to herself. He was come! How could she have doubted but that he would?!

She rose to her feet and turned to face him but—what was this? He was not smiling. In fact he looked quite sad. Her heart began to sink within her, and she bit her lip nervously.

"Miss Sophie, I have heard the sad news of your recent disappointment. May I extend my sympathy and sincere condolences?"

"What sad news?" asked Sophie, plainly puzzled.

"I understand your fiancé cast you away."

It angered her that he should regard her as an object of pity. "Really, my lord, I can assure you it was a mutual desire on both our parts. Will you be kind enough to escort me to my horse? My sister appears to have deserted me."

"I sent her packing."

"You had your nerve!" she exclaimed, fighting back her tears.

He came to stand very close to her. "If you wish to cry, I should be pleased to lend you my shoulder."

"I am not about to cry," she said, tears slowly gliding down her cheeks.

"Is it this Oliver you weep for?"

"I tell you I am not crying!" she said with a sob.

His arms came up and enfolded her. "There, there, it is not so bad as all that. He did not sound a proper husband for you. You are well rid of the fellow."

It was wonderful! In his arms she had not the least desire to weep. She looked up into his face and studied his eyes for a brief moment, her lips trembling in a little smile.

The smile broadened and lit up her eyes as she said: "Yes, my lord, quite—especially since I have got me an earl, methinks."

His face came very close to hers and he murmured. "Aye, that you have, my love."

They were as close as close can be and were staring into each other's eyes, completely engrossed in the messages they were discovering.

"Oh, John!" cried Sophie softly, her arms tightening about his neck.

There was no resistance. His lips came to join with hers, and they were clinging to each other, their only wish—that it should never end.

* * *

Lord Dalby turned away from the window through which he had been peering, while a lively conversation was being enjoyed by the little group gathered in Lady Leighton's sitting room. He could see the path that led to the stables. Strolling toward the house was a couple, holding hands and gazing soulfully into each other's eyes as they walked and talked.

"May I have your attention!" he said loudly.

"Do you see them?" cried Sarah, running to the window with Percy right behind her.

"How do they appear?" asked the dowager.

"Like a pair of doves, billing and cooing!" exclaimed Sarah, turning to face them all, a gleeful look on her features.

"I sincerely pray that this is the end of the mischief," declared Lady Dalby. "I do not think I can stand much more."

"And I pray that all will be quickly settled and my clerk can begin to work with me," said Lord Dalby.

"Oh, I say, my lord!" exclaimed Percy, a troubled look on his face. "It cannot be all that soon, don't you know? I mean to say there is the wedding to be got through and then there is the wedding trip—the honeymoon—to be got through—"

"I like that, I do!" cried Sarah. "You make it sound a positive chore!"

"Oh, I never meant it to sound that way, my love!" protested Percy as Sarah dragged him off to a corner and began to lecture him.

Lord Dalby watched with a sour but amused expression. He muttered to Lady Dalby. "So much for my clerk! I had best start off for London immediately and begin a quest for a body to assist me—"

"What can you be thinking of, Alan?! Of course you will not do any such thing!" exclaimed Lady Dalby. "We have weighty matters to discuss—just as soon as your prospective brother-in-law and Sophie arrive. I am bound to see everything tied up neatly before we dare even to think of departing."

Lord Dalby looked troubled. "Oh, I say, Pennie, I realize how important all of this is to you, but the business of the King's Bench Court is, you will admit, a heavier business, since it does concern the nation."

"Alan, love, how would you feel if, for the lack of your presence, Sophie and John were not in a position to tie the knot?"

He scowled. "After what we have all been through, very poorly."

"I rest my case."

Into the room, all smiles, came Lord Leighton with Sophie clinging to his arm, her cheeks a pretty pink.

Very proudly, he announced: "My lady mother, my honored guests, I have the most wonderful news for you!"

Everyone burst into laughter as they came forward to congratulate the beaming couple.

If you have your heart set on Romance, read

Coventry Romances

THE TULIP TREE—Mary Ann Gibbs	50000–4	$1.75
THE HEARTBREAK TRIANGLE —Nora Hampton	50001–2	$1.75
HELENE—Leonora Blythe	50004–7	$1.75
MEGAN—Norma Lee Clark	50005–5	$1.75
DILEMMA IN DUET—Margaret SeBastian	50003–9	$1.75
THE ROMANTIC WIDOW —Mollie Chappell	50013–6	$1.75

*Let Coventry give you
a little old-fashioned romance.*

This offer expires 1/24/81   8000-3